OHIO
DOMINICAN
UNIVERSITY™

SINCE 1911

MY FATHER
THE WEREWOLF

Also by Henry Garfield
The Lost Voyage of John Cabot
Tartabull's Throw
Room 13
Moondog

MY FATHER
THE WEREWOLF

a novel by
HENRY GARFIELD

A RICHARD JACKSON BOOK
ATHENEUM BOOKS FOR YOUNG READERS
New York London Toronto Sydney

○ ☾ ● ⟩ ⟩ ○ ● ● ●

Atheneum Books for Young Readers • An imprint of Simon & Schuster Children's
Publishing Division • 1230 Avenue of the Americas, New York, New York 10020
This book is a work of fiction. Any references to historical events, real people, or real
locales are used fictitiously. Other names, characters, places, and incidents are products of
the author's imagination, and any resemblance to actual events or locales or
persons, living or dead, is entirely coincidental. • Copyright © 2005 by Henry Garfield
All rights reserved, including the right of reproduction in whole or in part in any form.
Book design by Sonia Chaghatzbanian • The text for this book is set in Sabon.
Manufactured in the United States of America • 10 9 8 7 6 5 4 3 2 1 • Library of Congress
Cataloging-in-Publication Data • Garfield, Henry. My father the werewolf / Henry
Garfield.—1st ed. • p. cm. • "A Richard Jackson Book." • Summary: Teenagers
Miranda and Danny move to Maine to be near a deserted island where their werewolf
father can isolate himself during full moons, but when the ocean freezes and creates a
path to the populated mainland, they resort to desperate measures to save the townspeople from their transformed parent. • ISBN 0-689-85180-4 • [1. Werewolves—
Fiction. 2. Fathers—Fiction. 3. Brothers and sisters—Fiction. 4. Family
problems—Fiction. 5. Maine—Fiction. 6. Horror stories.] I. Title. • PZ7.G17939My
2005 • [Fic]—dc22 • 200401059

To Elaine, whose love makes everything possible

Titanic, true love makes everyone beautiful.

MY FATHER
THE WEREWOLF

ONE

The old man had seen them from his cabin—the last cabin of its kind along this stretch of rolling dunes south of Pismo Beach. Both man and cabin had been here for a long time. Once Pismo had been a quiet little beach town between Los Angeles and San Francisco, a haven for artists and a few early hippies, and cabins like Sid's had dotted the shore where the cedar forest met the sand. That was before the tourists and the RV and dune-buggy crowds had discovered the place, and pushed most of Sid's kind farther north, or up into the hills. Sid McKenzie clung tenaciously to his little piece of California coast.

The fog caressed the land with long, lugubrious fingers, playing in and out of the shallow valleys between the hills that rolled to the shore. Sid knew the fog as an old friend. He knew its moods, its patterns, its movements. Sometimes in summer it rolled in from the ocean before nightfall, smothering everything in a wet gray blanket. Other times it teased and prodded and probed and danced along the contours of the coast, pulling back now and again to reveal the foam of wave tops and the sprinkled stars. Sid knew the moods of Pismo better than anyone. In his youth he had surfed here, on a long board made of pine, sanded and varnished and as lovingly maintained as any sailboat. The board now hung high up on a wall in his cabin. He had left Pismo during the height of the war in Vietnam. He had returned a year before the first full-moon murder. He didn't surf anymore. Now he kept watch.

Sid heard the family—a father and two kids—before he saw them. The girl and the boy were arguing, oblivious to their surroundings. Teenagers, from the sound of their voices and their vocabulary. The father trailed a short distance behind them, trying to stay out of the argument, interjecting only when one of the kids employed a particularly colorful phrase.

Not many people walked this far down the beach from the campground, but that was undoubtedly where they had come from, for there were no roads between here and there, and he could tell they weren't locals. The girl was of medium height, with long, blondish hair and a developing figure. She walked deliberately, striding up the sides of the dunes and pausing on top, hands on hips, waiting for the others. The son was the same height, but wiry, and more active. He had a mop of dark brown hair cut just above his eyebrows and ears, and he wore a black sweatshirt that was a couple of sizes too big for him. He covered twice as much ground as the other two, because while his father and sister walked methodically up each dune, hewing straight on in one direction, the boy described arcs and orbits around them both, running up the faces of dunes and then rolling down them, sometimes darting toward the ocean in pursuit of something interesting. City kids, Sid thought, happy to be away from thieves and muggers and rapists and pushers and prostitutes. Unaware, of course, of the danger that lurked among the dunes.

Sid knew. Three times he had come face-to-face with the werewolf of Pismo Beach. Once, he had taken a shot at it but the beast had gotten away.

Sometimes months would go by without an incident. Sometimes he would hear howls in the hills and find tracks the next morning, tracks that wouldn't last long in the shifting sand. Sid didn't know who the werewolf was in human form. He speculated that it might be a drifter who returned periodically to Pismo. But it had killed—oh, yes, it had killed. And was fully capable of killing again.

He watched as the family walked farther into the dunes. Soon they were swallowed up by the fog again. Slowly Sid rose and walked into his small cabin. From the wall beside the door he took down his rifle. From a drawer in an antique table he drew out a box of bullets. He returned to his chair on the porch and began to load the gun.

"Wow, I feel like I'm in the Sahara or something," Miranda said. The dunes rolled away from them into the fog in all directions. Far off, they could hear the surf, but the walls of the world were gray and darkening. The Sun had set, though they had not seen it.

"How far do you think we've walked?" Danny asked.

"Far enough for it to be quiet, finally," his father answered. Ken Paxton raised his arms and turned slowly in place, surveying the dunes. "I've never been to this part of the beach before."

"Well, we ought to be getting back," Miranda reminded him. "It's going to be dark soon."

"It's the longest day of the year," her father said. "The summer solstice. If we were in Alaska right now, the Sun wouldn't set until eleven o'clock. In Maine it's light till nine." He laughed at some private joke. "Some year I want to be way up north on the summer solstice. Watch the Sun circle the sky. I think I'd really feel that I was on the surface of a planet, turning and moving through space."

Danny and Miranda exchanged a look: Here he goes again.

They had come to Pismo for the weekend to

escape the crowds, but the campground had been filled to capacity by people with the same idea. "Let's go for a walk," their father had suggested, and they had ended up here, miles from town.

"I like this fog," he said now. "It reminds me of Maine."

"Everything reminds you of Maine," Miranda said.

Their father laughed. "I've been out in boats in this kind of stuff," he said, looking off into nothing, remembering his youth on another ocean.

"It's pretty nice here," Miranda said, a trifle defensively.

Ken Paxton turned toward the sound of the pounding surf and inhaled a mouthful of moist air. "Yeah, you're right. It really is." He draped an arm over the shoulder of each child; Danny wriggled a bit but Miranda didn't mind. "Things are gonna get better," he said. "You wait. It's gonna get better. Let's head back."

A moderate wind had already begun to erase their footprints. Overhead a few bright stars peeked out from holes in the fog, and to the east they could see the outlines of the hills behind the shore. On the beach, though, the gray mist surrounded them. They could not see the water, nor more than a few yards up and down the coast in either direction.

"Dad," Danny said suddenly. "What's that light over there?"

He pointed toward the hills. A fuzzy, circular light, obscured by the lip of the fog bank, emanated from a low spot between ridges. It looked at first like some kind of searchlight. But the light shone steadily even as the fog moved. After long seconds Ken realized what it was.

"It's the Moon," he told his son. "The full moon. It's just rising."

Sounds travel well in fog, and Sid McKenzie heard Danny and Miranda arguing long before they came back into view. "The ocean's right there, you dork," the girl said. "Of course you can hear it. You don't need to hold a shell up to your ear."

"You're just mad 'cause I saw it first," her brother shot back.

"Let me hold it."

"No! It's mine—I found it."

"I just want to see it for a minute. Dad, Danny won't let me look at the shell he found."

"See it? It's right here in my hand."

"Dad!"

"I fail to see how this involves me," their father said.

"Let me hold it," Miranda insisted.

"No! You'll break it!"

"How's she going to do that?" their father interjected. "By dropping it in the sand?"

"Just let me see it for a friggin' minute," Miranda said.

"Well, okay, but give it right back." Reluctantly Danny placed the fist-sized moon shell in his sister's hands.

Instantly she ran off with it, to the top of a nearby dune. "Ha! It's mine now," she cried, waving the shell in the air.

"Miranda!" Danny climbed up the face of the dune, flailing his arms and screaming his indignation, giving his sister exactly the reaction she wanted.

"Jeez Louise, you'd think you guys were five and six years old the way you carry on," Ken said, exasperated. "Miranda, give him back his shell. And Danny, stop making all that noise."

"Who's gonna hear us, way out here?" Miranda said.

"Give him back his shell." He stared at her for emphasis. After several defiant seconds she lowered her eyes.

"Here's your stupid shell," she said, flipping the shell in a small arc just out of Danny's reach. Danny lunged in the sand for it; the shell landed unharmed inches beyond his outstretched arms.

"God, I get sick of the way you two squabble all the time," their father said. "It's bad enough that I have to listen to it. You come to a beautiful place like this, and all you can do is fight with each other. You think anyone wants to hear it?"

"Dad, look around," Miranda said. "Nobody can hear us."

But Sid McKenzie, hidden from them by the dunes and the darkness, could hear them quite clearly. And he knew that his were not the only

9

ears attuned to the intruders. It was out here with them, somewhere close. The old man could sense its presence.

Not many campers were foolish enough to walk this far away from the campground in the gathering darkness, and fewer still chose to do so when the Moon was full. The locals were even more cautious. There were stories, and though most professed not to believe them, this part of the beach remained uncrowded.

Now the glowing orb rose above the hills, and the wisps of the low-lying fog could not conceal it entirely. Sid gripped the rifle and followed the family at a safe distance.

Five pelicans in formation wheeled in the fog and dipped toward the dunes to check the humans out. Danny whooped, arms pinwheeling, as the pelicans turned easily and glided away toward the surf. He and Miranda, recently released from the confines of school and city, raced after them. Their father watched them go, a thin smile on his lips. The Moon rose out of the wispy fog, and something moved in the trees behind him.

Ken didn't see it, for he was watching his kids and the birds and the waves of fog as they rolled along the waves of sand. But Sid McKenzie raised his rifle to his shoulder and squinted through the telescopic sight. The animal crouched at the edge of the woods, its yellow eyes intent, its ears flattened along its elongated skull. Sid held his breath. He'd never had such a good look at it. Its fur was blacker than the night; its shoulders hunched with coiled power. The werewolf of Pismo Beach, whose very existence would have been hotly denied by the responsible citizenry of the town, was his.

But then the man, still unaware of the beast's presence, took a couple of casual steps in the sand and put himself directly between Sid and his quarry. "Damn," the old man whispered to himself. "He's right in my line of fire!"

The kids were far to seaward now, almost to the shore, oblivious to the danger. Their cries reached Sid's ears like something from another universe, unconnected to the moment. The whole of his attention was focused on the eyes of the werewolf, and he saw the moment of decision in the creature's eyes. Sid was out from behind the dune and running toward the man even as the werewolf sprang from its cover and attacked.

The beast leaped at its prey, sending him sprawling face first in the sand. Ken barely had time to turn over before the werewolf was upon him. He flung his arms up in front of his face and screamed as the beast's jaws opened. The werewolf sank its teeth into Ken's left shoulder, inches from his throat.

Sid McKenzie cried out too, as he flew across the dunes with a speed belying his years. He raised the rifle like a baseball bat and swung it at the werewolf's head. It landed with a crack.

Momentarily stunned, the beast released the bleeding man and turned on its attacker. Sid backed away, fumbling with the rifle, certain he was staring into the face of his own death. And then the man who had just been bitten did an amazing thing. With his uninjured arm he reached down, grabbed a handful of sand, and flung it in the werewolf's face. The creature roared and turned on him.

Sid's hands furiously worked the rifle's firing mechanism. He rolled and aimed the rifle upward. There was no time for precision. He squeezed the trigger.

Sand kicked up around him in the gun's recoil. The beast screamed and staggered backward. Sid cocked the rifle and prepared to fire again. The werewolf roared, and then turned and ran on all fours back into the trees.

Suddenly the only sound was the white noise of the distant surf. Sid lay on the sand, hands gripping the rifle hard, his aging heart hammering in his chest. Then he heard a moan. Sid raised his head, and with an effort he got to his feet and went over to the fallen man.

Danny and Miranda had heard the shot and came quickly. They stopped when they saw their father bleeding in the sand, with a strange old man huddled over him. The old man looked up at them. "Help me," he said.

The girl crouched in the sand beside her father. Her wide-eyed brother pulled up, panting, behind her. But Ken's eyes were clear, not glazed with shock. "He's going to be okay," Sid said. "I scared it off." Then to the father: "Unbutton your shirt, so I can take a look."

"What happened, Dad?" Danny asked.

"A dog bit me," Ken said, fumbling with his buttons.

"No dog," Sid said, helping Ken draw back the shirt to examine the wound. "But you got bit, all right."

"By what?" Miranda asked. She too was looking at the wound—a series of ragged punctures between neck and shoulder. Several of the teeth marks seeped blood; Ken's hand and most of his shirtfront were stained red. But he was breathing normally, and he allowed the old man to help him to his feet.

"I winged him," the old man said, casting a glance at the trees. "Damn, I wish I'd had a clear shot." He turned his attention back to Ken. "I'll take you to my place, so we can dress that," he said. "It's not far."

The cabin, though roomy enough for one person, felt small with all of them in it. Heavy wooden beams ran beneath a high cathedral ceiling and a partially enclosed loft where the old man slept. The lower level surrounded a central fireplace and chimney. The walls were dark wood. The cabin's interior was festooned with silver. A shiny crucifix hung from a television antenna bent just so to bear its weight. Silver candlesticks and figurines lined the shelves between books on surfing, the occult, and the central California coast. Wreaths of garlic decorated the tiny kitchen area and gave it fragrance. A large pentagram was painted on one wall in red.

Sid built up the fire and made hot chocolate for everybody, splashing some brandy in his own and Ken's. He boiled water, took some dried leaves down from a cabinet, and made a poultice for the father's injured shoulder. Ken relaxed against the back of the couch and sipped his drink.

Miranda looked anxiously at the old man. "Will Dad be okay?" she asked.

"Of course I'll be okay, honey," Ken said, attempting a reassuring smile. "It's just a dog bite."

"But you said it wasn't a dog," Miranda said, still looking at Sid.

The old man said nothing.

"If it wasn't a dog, what was it?"

The old man's eyes shifted from father to daughter and back again. "Your father was bitten by a werewolf, Miranda."

"I don't believe it!" Miranda cried.

"Believe it," Sid said grimly. "I wounded him once before too, I think. In the leg. Spent the next month skulking around town looking for anyone with a limp."

Danny was dumbstruck. "How long—"

"How long has he been here?" Sid asked. Miranda and Danny nodded.

"Almost ten years now," the old man said, answering his own question. "But he comes and goes. He disappears for months at a time. He's killed four people so far, that I know of." Sid looked pointedly at Ken. "You're lucky you weren't the fifth."

"What's going to happen to him?" Miranda asked, leaning forward, her empty cup between her knees.

Sid McKenzie paused before replying. "Child, you must know"—he stopped, aware that all three of his guests were looking at him intently—"that is, well . . . A person who is bitten by a werewolf, and survives, becomes a werewolf." He looked at Ken. "A month from now, on the next full moon, that's when you'll change," he said. "And every full moon thereafter."

Ken let this sink in for a moment. "You are telling me," he said slowly, "that I am now a werewolf?"

The old man gave him a solemn nod. "I'm afraid that's about the size of it."

"I can't believe this," Danny said.

The old man's eyes flicked to the boy briefly, then returned to his sister.

"Isn't there anything we can do?" Miranda said.

The old man shook his head. "Keep track of the calendar," he said. "Full moon happens at a specific moment, but there's a period of about three nights when the Moon is full enough to bring on the transformation. You'll have to make sure

17

your father isn't in a position to do anybody any harm. Beyond that, you would have to trace the bloodline of the werewolf that bit him, and kill off every werewolf in the chain. And I wouldn't even know where to begin."

"But you knew he was out here!" Danny cried. "You knew! And you let him bite my dad!"

"I'm sorry. I was too late to stop it. I couldn't get a clear shot."

No one said anything for a long moment. Miranda and Danny exchanged fierce glances, but for once, they had nothing to say to each other.

At length the old man spoke again. "You'll have to take precautions, of course," he said.

TWO

Perhaps they would have moved to Maine anyway, even if it hadn't happened, because their father had been going on about it for the last few years. He hated the crowds in California. He complained about them to his Maine family during summer visits. A couple of years earlier they had gone swimming with Aunt Bonnie and their cousins Derek and Bobby (named after their aunt's two favorite hockey players, Derek Sanderson and Bobby Orr), and their father couldn't get over being alone on the beach in July. Danny and Miranda both thought it was a scruffy little beach, filled with rocks and mussel shells instead of sand, and the water was freezing, but Ken still marveled that nobody else was there.

The night after they returned home from Pismo Beach, he pulled out a map of Maine and pointed to a spot halfway up the coast. "Liverpool," he said. "Named after the town in England the Beatles came from. It's got a harbor, and more importantly, there's a twenty-acre island at the mouth of the harbor. Too far to swim, but you can get there in a small boat."

Ken had explored it as a boy. No one lived there, and you could go out and walk around. There was an old foundation and a crumbling dock made of stone pilings. The island was wooded, and supported deer and smaller animal life. It was called, naturally enough, Harbor Island.

When school got out a few days later, Danny and Miranda went to stay with their mother for a couple of weeks, and two days after the next full moon Danny read a story in the newspaper about three illegal immigrants who had been attacked and killed in the desert by some wild animal as they were trying to make their way into the United States. He showed the article to his sister. "It could have been him," Miranda whispered. "Or it might have been a mountain lion." They agreed not to say anything to either of their parents. When their father came to pick them up, he looked fine, except for a thin scratch across his forehead that was already healing.

Danny asked him how it got there, and his father said, "Tree branch, I think. I don't know. I don't really remember."

"Did you turn, um, into a werewolf, like the old man said?" Danny asked.

Ken shook his head. "I don't remember that, either," he said. "I went out into the desert, slept under the stars, away from civilization. Had a bunch of strange dreams."

Danny and Miranda looked at each other across the back of the car seat, a silent, terrible question hanging between them.

"I'm thinking about going back east," their father said. "Getting out of California."

At first Danny and Miranda thought about living

with their mother rather than letting their father drag them across the country to a place they barely knew, but Barbara Paxton settled the issue by going off on one of her binges two weeks before the August full moon. This time she was gone for only three days, but that was long enough for their father to decide. He couldn't hide out in the desert every time the Moon was full, and he couldn't count on his ex to take care of Danny and Miranda when his time of the month rolled around.

Their father had wanted to leave California ever since Danny and Miranda had come to live with him, a year after the divorce and two weeks after their mom had wrecked her car and lost her driver's license for her third drunk-driving arrest. Danny and Miranda had lived through his struggles, from job to job, from house to apartment to even smaller apartment, where their dad didn't even have his own bedroom, but slept on the living-room couch.

Like so many other people who come to Southern California, he harbored aspirations of writing for the movies. And their father had gotten further than most. He had actually completed a screenplay and found an agent. Moreover, the agent had secured an option for his screenplay, entitled *Riders of the Purple Dawn,* for ten thousand dollars. The option had been dropped after a year but the agent was still hopeful, and encouraged Ken to write another one.

"I can write in Maine as well as I can in California," he said. "And it's not so damned expensive to live there." Becoming a werewolf had confirmed the notion.

"What about school?" Miranda asked anxiously.

"You can go to school in Liverpool," their father said. "The schools in California are going to hell anyway."

Danny and Miranda didn't argue with this. Miranda was sixteen and would be a junior; Danny, a year and a half younger, would be a freshman. The school they attended was switching to a year-round schedule in the fall because of overcrowding, and had already mandated school uniforms in an effort to forestall gang violence. Though Danny and his sister didn't like either of these changes, they liked even less the idea of attending a strange school on the other side of the country.

But their father's mind was made up. The rent on their tiny, cramped apartment was a month past due anyway. Ken didn't bother to pay it. He got extra hours at his telemarketing job, bought a trailer hitch for the van, arranged to rent a U-Haul trailer, and told Danny and Miranda to say good-bye to their friends.

Their mother took the news with remarkable calm. Danny and his sister expected a scene, but Mom put on a big dinner the night they left, stayed sober the whole time, and gave them each a big hug and a kiss and a box of stationery and told them to write lots of letters.

Twenty-four hours later Miranda bade a tearful good-bye to her friend Jenny, Ken beat Jenny's father in a final game of chess, and they locked up the U-Haul and rolled onto the freeway and up into the mountains. There had been no tears between Danny and his friends. They had spent one final evening illegally skateboarding around a construction site, watching out for cops, and then that world and the people in it were gone, to be replaced with whatever lay over the horizon.

"After the Continental Divide it's all downhill," Ken said cheerfully, as the van groaned past the freeway sign declaring four thousand feet of elevation. He was glad to go, Danny could tell, whatever lay ahead. The Moon, not quite full, loomed over the mountaintops, yellow in the east, pointing the way out of California. They left their mother's house before midnight and reached the Colorado River by dawn.

It got hot the minute the Sun came up. Not that it had been very cool at night—Ken stopped once at a little intersection to get a Coke out of a machine outside a store, and they could feel the heat rising off the desert even at three in the morning. A bunch of truckers had stopped there as well, to catch their breath. The air smelled of creosote and exhaust; a warm wind stirred it around, but there was no relief in it, just hot air moving from one part of the desert to another.

The fact of the river in all that blasted emptiness

was sort of amazing, and Danny could see why modern civilization had almost sucked the Colorado dry. A hundred miles in either direction was a cruel land of cacti and flat rocks and ocotillo, where men died, and still do, of thirst and heatstroke. The Colorado was cool and deep and blue, and moved rapidly past Needles, the last town in California, where they stopped. There were seventeen dams on the Colorado, Danny had read somewhere. Cities from Denver to Los Angeles dipped their straws in. What must it have looked like to the early pioneers, who had staggered across the waterless desert to stand on its banks? It must have seemed like a miracle.

They found a park by the river's edge, and Danny and Miranda went swimming while their father caught a couple hours of sleep in the back of the van.

Miranda had taken driver's ed that year and practiced with the van a lot, though she didn't have her permit yet. "What do you think he'd do if we drove off right now, and he woke up fifty miles down the road, with me driving?" she said.

"What's he going to do tonight?" Danny countered. "You saw the Moon . . ."

"I know." Miranda looked at him seriously. "Do you believe it, Danny? The old man, the werewolf stuff? Do you honestly believe that when the Moon rises, Dad's going to turn into some blood-crazed beast?"

He thought about it for a minute. "I don't know," he finally said. He didn't want to believe it. He didn't want his father to believe it. But if he didn't, why were they suddenly moving across the country, before another full moon rose over California? Had he killed those people out in the desert?

Their father started to plan aloud halfway across Arizona. Danny sat in the back and played with his Game Boy and didn't say much. They stopped for lunch in Flagstaff, at a Mexican place. Two middle-aged Native American women sold jewelry at a table in the lobby. When they left the restaurant, Ken stopped to talk to them and purchased two items.

He gave these to Danny and Miranda an hour later, at the meteor crater, the same one that was in

Danny's seventh-grade science textbook. Two small, identical silver pentagrams on silver chains. "Put these on," he said. "Tonight's the first night. We'll find a place away from people."

"That shouldn't be hard," Miranda said, looking around. There had been trees in Flagstaff, but here the desert stretched, empty and open, to the horizon. "Then what?"

"You guys sleep in the van, with the doors locked. I'll get as far away as possible. And just to be safe, Miranda, I'll give you the keys. You can drive in an emergency."

Miranda nodded solemnly and looked out at the opposite rim of the crater. They had camped before, of course. And Dad liked to camp in unauthorized places, which he called "guerrilla camping"—a term that confused Danny at first until his father explained that it had nothing to do with the gorillas that live in the jungle and eat grubs. But this was new. This was different. Their father had always camped with them. Now he was proposing to leave them out alone in the desert while he went off somewhere and turned into a werewolf.

They drove on, listening to music but not saying much, and as the afternoon ran out, so did Arizona. Near the New Mexico border, the scrub grass desert gave way to red bluffs overlooking a mostly dry riverbed. Clouds had welled up in front of them, and as they crossed from one state into the next, suddenly it was dark and gray. A moment later big raindrops began to splatter on the windshield, and minutes after that they could see no more than a few car lengths ahead of them in a torrential downpour. Ken had the wipers going full speed as the rain pelted down. Still he could barely see. And it kept coming down—it wasn't a short, violent cloudburst that spends itself all in one blast and leaves a rainbow. This was a monsoon.

"I guess we can forget camping tonight," Ken said.

He pulled off at the next exit. Gallup, New Mexico, seemed like an endless strip of gas stations, fast-food restaurants, and motels. "One long necklace of neon gems," their father said. "Glittering logos of corporate America."

Danny didn't see what was so bad about it. You could have set Gallup's main drag down anywhere in San Diego, and the city would have swallowed it up.

Ken drove past the Holiday Inn and the Best Western and most of the strip before pulling in at the cheesiest motel he could find, advertising single-occupancy rooms for $19.95 on a sign with several letters missing. The rain was still coming down in sheets. Ken ran into the office, transacted business, ran out, and drove the van to the door of room number eight, at the edge of a paved courtyard.

The room had one light, a tall lamp that they had to drag into the bathroom because the lights there were all out. But the shower worked, and so did the TV, although it got only two channels. And as long as the sky kept raining—or stayed overcast, for that matter—their father was safe from the full moon, and Miranda and Danny were safe from him.

He got up and went out sometime after midnight. He was back by dawn, and he looked okay. Outside, the sky was still gray. He hadn't changed, he said. He went to a couple of late-night bars, had a couple of drinks, then spent the rest of the night walking around Gallup after it stopped raining.

"He took a big chance," Danny said to his sister, as their father napped on one of the large beds. "What if the Moon had come out while he was sitting in one of those bars?"

"Would've put Gallup, New Mexico, on the map," she replied.

As soon as they left Gallup, the Sun came out. Danny had never seen such openness. The mountains loomed like far-off sentries; they kept their distance from one another so that the feeling was one of traveling between, not among them. High clouds swept across the sky, and the sides of the mountains were green. And always he had the awareness of altitude. They stopped at the Continental Divide, where their father made a big deal of taking a leak on the spot and telling them that he was pissing into two oceans at once. They were 7,500 feet above sea level. By late afternoon they went higher still, across Raton Pass, into Colorado, the van struggling to pull the trailer over the top.

By this time their father had reconsidered the whole notion of guerrilla camping. Instead he checked into a motel in Trinidad, the first town in

Colorado, ordered a pizza, and prepared to head out in the van by himself. "What will you do?" Danny asked him.

His father took out the map and pointed to a highway running along the bottom of Colorado. "I've been through this way before," he said. "There's nothing between here and Kansas. Nothing but open plains."

What he planned to do, he said, was drive about thirty miles out of Trinidad, bury the keys under a rock, and walk as far out into the open prairie as he could before the Moon rose. He would return to pick them up in the morning.

When he left, Danny and Miranda talked about calling their mother and telling her everything—that Dad was convinced he had become a werewolf and that he had left them alone in a motel in Colorado. They wondered why he hadn't waited to make the trip until the Moon cycled past full. It was obvious that he didn't trust Mom to be around to take care of them during the full moon. They speculated for the thousandth time what it would be like to have functional, responsible parents.

They worried about the kind of life they would have in Maine. They watched the Moon rise over the Spanish architecture of the town from their motel window. Then they watched *Beavis and Butt-Head Do America* on HBO, which came free with the room.

Ken didn't come back until nine in the morning, after it had been light out for hours. Miranda was still sleeping, but Danny was wide awake and worried. Their father had run miles from the car and it had taken him hours to find it again, he said, but he looked happy. Tired, but happy. He had ripped one shirtsleeve, but there were no bloodstains on his clothes, and though he needed a shower, there was no smell of death about him. The plan had worked. They went out for breakfast to celebrate. Dad had steak and eggs, with an English muffin and a huge helping of hash browns on the side, and he polished off every bit of it. Danny had scrambled eggs and gave Dad his last piece of bacon when he caught him eyeing it. Miranda had a fruit plate and regarded them both with disgust.

Trinidad was a pretty town, the last gasp (or first glimpse, depending on which direction you were going) of the Southwest. They lingered until almost noon, admiring the stone streets and old buildings set against the red mountains. An hour into the day's drive, the mountains were gone, replaced by an endless plain and a razor-straight highway that stretched to the horizon. They would not see a hill of any appreciable size until they reached Pennsylvania several days later, when the Moon would be safely waning.

But here it would be full one more night, and Ken tried to time the drive so that dusk would not catch them near any centers of population. They stopped at some sort of street fair in Dodge City, Kansas, where Danny and Ken ate ostrich burgers and endured Miranda's further disapproval.

"How can you be disgusted by ostrich burgers when you like Slim Jims and pepperoni pizza?" Danny asked her.

"I don't mind meat as long as it's well disguised," Miranda replied.

Before they got too close to Wichita, their dad

found another cheap motel, checked in and bought food, and lit out again for an empty spot on the map. "Last night of this," he promised when he left.

He looked pretty bad when he came in the next morning—Danny guessed the lack of sleep was beginning to tell. Another shower and another huge breakfast, and then they hit the road. They didn't get far, however. Before they were even out of Kansas, their father found a park by a little lake and promptly fell asleep in the back of the van for about five hours. Danny tried fishing in the lake but didn't catch anything.

They camped that night in Missouri. Dad said he couldn't keep shelling out money for motels now that the Moon was past full. It rose as they were roasting marshmallows over the coals of their campfire. Dad shuddered, and Danny and Miranda looked at him in alarm, but nothing else happened. The Moon was egg shaped; as it shrank it would rise later each night and linger in the morning sky during the rest of the trip across the continent.

Traveling through Missouri, they stopped at a huge fireworks store, where Danny blew most of the allowance he had saved for months. They had been seeing billboards for fireworks all across the state, and this store was unbelievable. It was a huge warehouse with liquor on one side and fireworks on the other. "I guess the big thing to do in Missouri is get drunk and blow things up," their father cracked. Danny ignored him. He was too busy looking at the Power Rockets—missiles as big as his arm that the sign said would fly three hundred feet in the air and do loop-de-loops as they exploded. Danny bought a big bag of firecrackers, several dozen exploding bees, a hundred-pack of Roman candles, some bottle rockets, a few cube-shaped devices that shot off multiple rounds of colored streamers, and six Power Rockets. The guy at the counter made Ken sign an agreement that they would use them responsibly.

"Man, I've never seen you so excited," Miranda said on their way back out to the van.

"Maine better watch out," Danny replied.

"Put them somewhere out of sight," his father said. "In case we get pulled over for speeding."

Danny knew that a lot of fathers wouldn't have

let their son buy such an arsenal. Dad was cool about fireworks. They appealed to his outlaw streak. So—unfortunately—did country music.

"I don't know what it is," Miranda said once, "but something in the human genetic code kicks in when a guy turns forty. Suddenly they respond to twangy voices, and fiddles, and cornball tales of their wives leaving them and their dogs dying." It was easy, they discovered, to find a country station on the radio no matter where you were in America. Danny and Miranda howled in protest whenever their dad dialed one in, but sometimes he shouted down their protests and made them listen until they could stand it no longer.

A prominent feature on a lot of those country stations, at least in the Midwest, was the farm report, where some laconic dude reported the latest hog prices and rainfall figures.

Their father was feeling good after his first night of solid sleep since California, and as they rolled toward the Mississippi River he was listening to a country station and tapping his fingers on the dashboard, a habit that drove Miranda nuts.

She was just about to tell him to cut it out when the farm report came on.

"Authorities have no new leads in the series of cattle mutilations that took place earlier this week in eastern Colorado and western Kansas," said the radio. Their father sat bolt upright and reached for the volume knob. "Fourteen animals were butchered and left to die over the course of two nights on two ranches approximately three hundred miles apart. Police have not determined whether the killings were the work of some kooky religious cult or a single deranged individual—"

There was more, but that was all their father needed to hear. The message was clear: He could run, but he couldn't hide.

It took four more days to get to Maine. They went to the Gateway Arch in St. Louis, camped along a mosquito-infested river in Indiana, and had a rear-end collision in Ohio with an elderly couple who stopped at a traffic light that was turning yellow. No one was injured, but Ken got a ticket and one of the van's headlights was useless for the remainder of the trip.

They skirted New York City and avoided Boston entirely, but they could not avoid the summer traffic on the Maine Turnpike. "I thought I left this behind in California," their father growled, and Danny wondered briefly if emotional stress could transform someone into a werewolf in broad daylight between full moons. In Portland they saw the Atlantic Ocean for the first time and abandoned the turnpike for Route 1, where, if anything, the traffic was worse. Two hours later, as dusk fell, they limped into Liverpool.

Danny had no strong first impressions of the town. After more than a week on the road they were all too tired to care. Their father wheeled the van and its attached U-Haul right into the center of town, between the old brick buildings that lined Main Street, through the abandoned rail yard and down to the waterfront. There were lots of boats in the harbor, and a touristy seafood restaurant out on the wharf. On the near side of the harbor, all lit up, was a large office building, surrounded by a fenced-in expanse of grass that no one seemed to be using. Out in the bay a lighthouse flashed red at five-second intervals. At the mouth of the harbor stood a wooded island. Gray cliffs rose from the sea and in turn were met by thick spruce forest. The island looked dark and uninhabited, but it provided shelter for Liverpool Harbor from the south. It served as both a landmark and a barrier.

"That's Harbor Island," their father said as they stood on the town wharf staring into the twilight. "Now all we need is a boat."

THREE

Many days later Harbor Island still looked unfriendly.
That was probably the reason, Danny decided, that
no one ever built a summer retreat on it, even though
it was within rowing distance of the mainland. The
island was once privately owned, their father had
told them, and men from Liverpool organized deer
hunting trips out there in November. But then the
island's owner died and left all twenty acres of it to
the Nature Conservancy. "That means no one can
build on it or cut down trees or exploit it in any
way," Ken explained.

Much of the island was ringed by cliffs, with
deep water right up close. The only place to land

was on the far side, where the rocks gave way to not a beach exactly, but a low spot dotted with boulders and a pebbly inlet big enough for a boat. You couldn't see a boat on the shore unless you really looked for it, and of course you couldn't see it from the town at all, because it was on the other side of the island.

"Boulder dead ahead," Miranda sang out from the bow as they approached the small landing area. Danny let the oars drag in the water and turned his head. Ken was making him row, because, he said, he'd have to do it eventually and needed to build up his endurance. Danny had agitated for an outboard motor, but his father said he didn't have the money, and besides, motors were more trouble than they were worth because they didn't start half the time. September was still like summer—not California summer, with ninety-degree days and no clouds— but still pretty warm. And a motor sure would have saved time, not to mention Danny's hands. His dad had him out practicing almost every day after school, and it didn't take long for him to develop a couple of fair-size blisters.

But there wasn't a lot to rowing, once you learned to dip your oars in straight and pull them smoothly through the water. The only time it sucked was when it was windy and the oars caught the tops of the waves and splashed cold water all over the boat. Dad's plan B, in case a storm kicked up around the time of the full moon, was to have Danny and Miranda lock him in the basement and go visit their grandparents, who lived farther Down East (in the direction of the prevailing wind, hence *down*wind, their father explained) along the Maine coast. Danny wondered how he planned to explain that one. *Could you take the kids for a few days while I turn into a werewolf?*

School was another thing. The kids here were different. Most of them had never seen a city the size of San Diego. Some of Danny's schoolmates talked about going deer hunting with their fathers and uncles and cousins, all of whom lived within a twenty-mile radius of Liverpool. None of the kids spiked their hair the way Danny had in California. The boys wore long pants even on the hottest days.

Danny coasted until he could see the boulder, a

cream-colored, cabin-size rock whose top lurked maybe four inches underwater. He dipped one oar in the water and held it there and the boat turned in that direction—a nifty trick he'd learned from his father. Dad had grown up around rowboats and had told Danny and Miranda that he did not remember learning how to row. "It's kind of like riding a bicycle," he'd said, and Danny had discovered to his relief that this was true. Anybody could do it.

"Rock off the starboard bow," Miranda cried, spotting a patch of seaweed floating up from its roots. She did that just to piss him off. Danny hadn't got this "port" and "starboard" stuff down yet. He knew port was left and starboard was right, but when you were facing backward in a rowboat you had to take a minute to think about it, and in the time you were thinking, you could hit something, like a rock. Danny bumped a couple of them on the way in, which no doubt pleased his sister.

It was nearly high tide, and Dad found an exposed tree root right on the shore. He secured the "painter," which is what they called the rope—no, the *line*—at the bow of the dinghy, though Danny couldn't see what it had to do with painting. Everything on a boat was called something else. Like the front was the "bow" and the back was the "stern." Why couldn't they just say right and left and front and back and rope, for God's sake?

"Ship the oars, son," Dad said, and Danny was tempted to give him a salute and say, "Aye, aye, Captain!" Something about boats made people weird, he concluded.

They dragged the dinghy a little way up onto the shore, even though it was tied, so it wouldn't bounce against the rocks and get more scratched up than it was. Dad had bought it used for a hundred bucks and it looked its age. The off-white fiberglass was dented and discolored and worn thin in places, but it didn't leak a drop, and it was a sturdy little boat, especially with three people in it. Danny could tell his father liked the idea of having a boat, and he could see this sort of glazed look come over his face every time they went out in it. His father also looked longingly at the sailboats in the harbor, and told Danny and Miranda about other islands he'd been to as a boy. Most of it didn't mean a thing to them. They were Californians.

From the mainland Harbor Island had looked like an impenetrable forest, but up close they could see that there were gaps between the trees and that they weren't all evergreens. Pieces of silver driftwood had been thrown up onto the bank by storm tides; there was also half a styrofoam lobster buoy, chopped by some boat's propeller, and a faded plastic motor oil container. There was no path as such; their father led them through the open areas between the trees, walking on a floor of moss and pine needles into the interior of the island. They had to climb over fallen limbs and push others out of the way as they went, but soon they emerged into a clearing filled with small trees and raspberry bushes. Ken stopped, and Danny and Miranda did too. It was perfectly quiet in there—you would never have known from the surroundings that you were on an island less than a mile from a town. They couldn't hear the ocean, or any cars on the mainland. The tops of the tall spruce trees that walled them in swayed in the wind. They couldn't feel the wind at all, down where they were.

Dad slowly turned, looking at everything, taking it in. Danny and his sister waited.

"It looks like no one's been here for a long, long time," he said.

"Why would anyone come?" Miranda said. "There's nothing out here but trees and pricker bushes."

"I don't know—to get away from the hustle and bustle of Liverpool," their father said.

Danny and Miranda both laughed. Liverpool's idea of congestion was two cars at a red light—and there were only two traffic lights in the whole town. Drive a mile off Route 1 and you were in the boonies. The people of Liverpool didn't need an island to get away from it all.

But Dad did. Danny watched him size the place up. He turned around slowly, then began walking away from them, toward two small birch trees near the edge of the clearing. The trees weren't that small, actually; when Danny and Miranda caught up to him, Dad had stopped at the edge of what was left of a house foundation, staring down at the two trees growing at the bottom of it.

Only two walls of the foundation were still standing, and large, shrub-filled cracks ran their length.
Fallen slabs of concrete lay covered with moss
around the bases of the two birches whose yellow-
tinged tops they had seen from across the clearing.
Several smaller trees and assorted bushes had also
taken root in the hole where the house had been.

"Someone lived here once," Miranda said.

"A penetrating glimpse into the obvious,"
Danny remarked.

"Shut up," Miranda said.

"Come on, kids," their father cut in. "I wonder
where the old dock was."

"Wouldn't it be on the side facing town?"
Danny asked.

"Worth a look," Dad said. "Although it could
have been that the island was settled before the
town was. A lot of islands in Maine used to be
inhabited and aren't anymore, now that the car
culture's taken over."

They bushwhacked through the trees and came
out on top of a moss-covered ledge some thirty feet
above the water of Liverpool Harbor. Directly

below them, small waves lapped at the foot of the cliff, which was actually made up of several huge slabs of granite, stacked one on top of the other. This whole side of the island was bald, and although the island itself offered protection from the sea, there was no sign that anyone had ever built a dock here. Perhaps their father was right. The long-ago residents, fishermen most likely, had looked outward to open ocean, rather than in toward the continent less than a mile away.

Danny tried to imagine what the harbor had looked like in colonial times. Certainly the high bridge across the mouth of the river that flowed into the bay, the bridge that carried truck traffic to Machias and Canada and trailerfuls of tourists to Acadia National Park and Greyhound buses to Bangor, had not been there. Nor had the fish cannery below it, the old brick buildings of downtown, and the houses up and down either shore with porches angled for optimum views of the water. And certainly the AMIC credit card company, built on a bit of land that bellied out into the harbor and thus was the closest piece of mainland to the island, had not been there. It had not been there even five years ago—Danny knew this from Eric, his new friend at school—and even from a distance it looked grafted onto the town, as out of place as the Klingon warship that Kirk and crew land in twentieth-century San Francisco in the *Star Trek* movie about the whales.

The main AMIC building was rectangular, with curved corners and long windows tinted gray, the kind through which you can see out, but not in. A smaller building, identical except in size, lay to the right of it across an expanse of grass along the shore. Everything they built was silver and blue— their buildings, fences, and the signs around the area that marked the property they were buying up. AMIC didn't use the waterfront except to look at; there was a fence along the shore, and a small deck directly in front of the building, but no docks or anywhere to land a boat. The docks were farther up the harbor, toward the fish plant—the town docks where the sightseeing boats landed, a boat-yard, and then the working docks of the cannery. What made AMIC look so out of place was the fact that it could have just as easily been in Nebraska.

The waterfront site on which AMIC's too-pristine building stood had once held a chicken-processing plant, and tourists to the Maine coast had avoided Liverpool because of the smell and the sight of chicken innards floating in the harbor and feathers blowing down the street. When the plant closed, a good chunk of Liverpool's economy had shut down too, and the town struggled through several years of depression before the Maryland-based credit card company bought the land and announced plans to open a major new customer service center. The company had billions of dollars at its disposal, didn't pollute the air or the water, and promised to eventually bring several thousand new jobs to the area, mostly in telemarketing—AMIC believed in aggressively calling its customers and persuading them to consolidate their debts from other credit cards into their AMIC accounts.

The Paxtons had settled on a house the first day. Their father wanted to be near the shore and near the town, and they found a funky little place with three bedrooms and a big front porch that needed fixing up and was for sale to anyone who wanted a project. The owner was moving to New Jersey and decided to rent out the house until she found a buyer. Ken signed a year's lease on the spot. Rentals were scarce, he learned, because AMIC kept hiring people from out of town who scooped them all up. Some people drove fifty or more miles to their jobs because they couldn't find an inexpensive rental in Liverpool.

Within a week Ken was working at the local cannery, getting up at six in the morning to report to work at seven. He got paid every Friday, and after his second paycheck he had enough money to buy the used dinghy.

"Maybe I should apply for a job at AMIC," he said now, looking back at the harbor. "I could do that. I was a telemarketer in San Diego, after all. It sucks, but I can do it."

"You know what AMIC stands for?" Miranda said.

"Uh-uh," their father replied. "Associated Maryland International Creditors, something like that."

Miranda shook her head. "My friend Nora told me," she said. "Her brother worked there the summer before he went to college. He said it stands for 'Assholes of Maine in Cubicles.'"

Their father laughed, and draped an arm across the shoulders of each of his children. They stood there for a long time, staring across the water at the strange little town that had suddenly become their home.

"Well, it'd be a hell of a swim," Ken said finally.

"You couldn't swim that," Miranda protested. "You'd freeze to death before you got to shore."

"Did you ever hear about the elephant who started swimming across the river, got three quarters of the way across, decided he couldn't make it, and turned around?"

"That's stupid," Miranda said.

"Can werewolves swim?" Danny asked.

"I don't know," their father said.

"Dogs can swim," Miranda said. "So can wolves."

"We had dogs when I was a kid," their dad said. "And puppies. Once I took a puppy, maybe six weeks old, waded out into the water until I was about waist deep, and let it go. The dog had never been in the water before. Had never *seen* the water. I wanted to find out if it had to *learn* to swim, or if it could do it by instinct."

"And did it?" Danny asked.

His father nodded. "Started dog-paddling toward the shore the minute I let go of it. Like it had been swimming for years."

"Still a pretty long swim," Miranda said, looking at the town and the AMIC complex.

"I know, and the water's freezing," Dad said. "Come on, let's get back to the boat."

They trudged through the interior of the island, breaking branches as they went, not saying much, preoccupied with private anxieties about the strangeness of their situation and the events that had led them from their crowded but comfortable neighborhood in San Diego to a deserted island on the coast of Maine. The September full moon was only three days away.

Danny came out into the clearing, and something jumped from the underbrush in front of him.

He and Miranda stopped, startled, but Dad took a few steps forward as a small, brown, furry shape bounded away from them and was gone. Then he looked back at them and laughed.

"Don't tell me you guys are scared of a rabbit," he said.

Danny and his sister were unused to things jumping up at them from underfoot, unless it was a street person in a doorway who suddenly regained consciousness to ask for change. Feeling sheepish, they continued through the clearing.

"Well, at least there's wildlife," Dad said. "Less incentive to swim to the mainland."

Miranda laughed. Danny and his father looked at her.

"What?" Danny said.

"Oh, I was just thinking about that movie *Never Cry Wolf*," she said. "How it turns out the wolves eat mice, mostly. Dad's gonna be a werewolf that chases rabbits. Not really the image most people have in mind."

"Be serious, Miranda. Better rabbits than human beings," her dad said. "We're damn lucky to find this place. It looks like nobody's been out here in months, maybe all summer. No one's gonna notice a few dead rabbits."

"Eric said there's deer out here too," Danny reminded him.

"All the better," Dad said. "Keep me busy, I mean," he added, when Miranda looked at him strangely. "Don't worry. It's gonna be all right. We couldn't have found a better place. I won't hurt anybody out here, 'cause there's no one out here to hurt. It's perfect. Perfect."

Their father rowed them to the mainland. He put his back into it, and they crossed quickly. Danny hadn't seen him so happy since before the trip to Pismo Beach. He believed he was free again. Not free from the curse, but from the pressure he had felt in California. He was a werewolf, yes, he said, but for the first time, after that first trip to Harbor Island, he felt like he could live with it, and the world could live with him.

FOUR

"I'm too old for this," Ken mumbled, as he passed Carlton with another slab of frozen fish. His friend nodded and groaned in sympathy.

The other three guys on the cannery crew didn't look any happier than he was about the prospect of staying late. All afternoon they had been unloading great slabs of frozen herring into the vats, tearing down each pallet and unwrapping each icy box before heaving the frozen bricks high over their heads and into the tubs of circulating water. If they landed flat, as they often did, water would splash up over the edges of the steel tubs. They were all tired, wet, and smelled like fish. The supervisor, a short guy with wire-rimmed glasses and a ponytail that stuck out the back of the baseball cap he wore over his hairnet, drove the forklift and helped cut the packages apart, but he claimed he wasn't strong enough to lift the ice chunks. The kid was maybe twenty-five, Ken surmised, and was their supervisor by virtue of seniority that could be counted in months. The four guys doing the actual work had all started that week.

"If he'd help, it'd go a hell of a lot faster," Carlton grumbled as he and Ken passed each other again. Ken slid another slab off the pile, straightened his legs, and carried it toward the vat they were now filling. The slabs were the size of small suitcases and must have weighed fifty pounds. Ken dropped his slab onto the concrete floor and stooped to pick it up. They were all wearing rubber boots and rubber gloves. Carlton was the biggest of the four of them and in decent physical shape, but even he found the work exhausting. At first this chore had seemed a welcome break from the monotony of the fish-packing line upstairs, but now they were all regretting the opportunity. If they had stayed on the line, they'd be getting out at three-thirty, the regular quitting time, instead of throwing around fifty-pound bricks of dead fish.

At least it's a little bit of extra money, Ken thought, even though the work was brutally hard. His back would ache tonight, and it would still hurt in the morning when he got up to do this all over again. His co-workers were all much younger—kids, really—except for Carlton. He looked like he'd been around some, and Ken was grateful to have someone to talk to.

Carlton Reynolds was thirty-three. He'd left Maine right out of high school, struck out on his own and picked up construction work in Florida, hitched west on the rumor of another job in Arizona, and got swept up in a drug bust in Phoenix when he was one of about a dozen people apprehended in a house with approximately a ton of marijuana behind the door of a bedroom. He worked six months on a road crew through the scorching desert summer; his skin blistered and he tanned so dark he looked like a Mexican. By the following spring he was back in Maine, working the first of a series of jobs like this one and dealing a little dope to meet expenses. He had a double-wide trailer and a piece of land and a live-in girl-friend with two kids and another on the way; he went deer hunting in the fall and played softball at the American Legion in the summer. His extended family was scattered all around the area, and he had friends from high school he still saw from time to time. If you could cut wood and shoot a gun, you could carve out a decent life in Maine, and his home state didn't attract weirdos of the kind he'd known in Florida and Arizona. Carlton was not an ambitious man, but he knew the value of work and respected it. "Anyone around here who doesn't have a job is just plain lazy," he'd told Ken the first morning on the packing line. "'Cause you can always work here."

The fish-packing plant was always hiring. If he stayed a month he'd get a fifty-dollar bonus; after three months he'd get another fifty; and after six months he'd get a hundred plus a week of paid vacation. There were always empty stations on the packing line; he'd read in the paper that the plant was operating at two-thirds capacity. Carlton knew, like everybody else, that the people who would have filled those jobs were being lured away by the AMIC corporation, that a lot of regular folks like himself had traded in their boots and blue jeans and hairnets for dress shoes and ties and had moved down the shore into a whole different world—the painfully tidy, blue-and-silver-trimmed world of badges and parking passes and security cameras. He saw kids who'd graduated years behind him driving brand new Camrys and Accords and going into the post office all dressed up, their bar-coded badges dangling proudly from the pocket flaps of their jackets even when they weren't at work. The Liverpool he'd left had been an ugly, impoverished factory town, but AMIC had brought something sterile and somehow sinister in its place. Carlton could not articulate this, but he felt it just the same, and it dismayed him when he heard about yet another former friend going to work there.

Hell, at least you can eat fish, he thought as he heaved another frozen slab into the vat. It was useful work that did some good in the world. Some of the people on the packing line were amazing. There was an Asian guy, tall like Carlton but with delicate hands like a woman's, who could pack eight cases of fish steaks an hour. A case was a hundred cans, stacked on wire trays of twenty-five. Packers were paid a dollar seventy a case or five fifty an hour, whichever was more. Carlton and Ken struggled to put up three cases in an hour, and in one late-afternoon flurry the day before, Carlton had almost done it. The Asian guy did eight, hour after hour, plucking fish from the table in front of him with both hands and placing them unerringly in the cans he'd lined up, filling whole rows of cans at once. Ken's fish kept popping out, causing him to swear under his breath and mash them back in, for the cans had to be packed tight because the fish condensed when cooked. He noticed that the Asian guy sat alone at break and simply stared into space as he ate. There was an old woman who bounced a leg to the beat of some interior song while she worked and packed almost as many cases as the Asian guy did.

In fact there were a lot of older women who could pack with lightning speed. "You won't make piecework your first week, maybe not even your first month," the woman who'd hired him had counseled. "It takes a while to get used to it."

But packing sucked, Carlton and Ken agreed. The steaks were the easiest—crosscut sections of fish, thumb size and teardrop shaped, that fit eight to a can, sometimes ten. You learned to do it two-handed, several cans at a time. The cans and fish came on two conveyor belts, one above the other; you placed the cans on the tray and scooped out fish onto the metal table in front of you. The fish and cans came constantly, so you had to keep up. The only breaks, other than the scheduled ones, came when they finished up one lot and started on another. Sardines, unlike the steaks, came whole except the head, and you had to tape your fingers and cut the tails off with scissors before laying the fish—four at a time, two with the black side up and two with the white side up—into the cans. Again, some of the people on the line who'd been there forever made blurs of the scissors and stacked up cases at a fair percentage of the speed of light, while Carlton nicked himself twice and had to do a whole tray over when the plump, schoolmarmish line boss passed his station and told him he'd been doing it wrong.

Fortunately (or so it had seemed at the time) she had approached Carlton that morning at six fifty-five and asked if he minded doing odd jobs around the factory once in a while instead of packing. He had said sure. Like an idiot.

Steve probably wouldn't wait for him, Carlton realized. He'd called last night, said he'd gotten some really good stuff, from New York, that Carlton could break down and sell for eighty dollars a quarter. He could use that money. Charlene and her kids were a constant litany of need, and now that she was pregnant with his own child, and out of work to boot, every penny counted. Even this job, at five fifty an hour, was better than nothing. He couldn't just blow it off, even though Steve was a better, if not more reliable, source of income.

"Take a break, boys," the little supervisor called at precisely three thirty, and Carlton set down the block of iced fish he'd just cut free. "Fifteen minutes." One thing he loved about blue-collar jobs, Carlton told Ken, was the sanctity of breaks. When it was time, it was time, period, and no matter what task you were in the middle of, you stopped right where you were and picked it up again when break ended. You were entitled to fifteen minutes every two hours, and by God everyone spent every second of those fifteen minutes determinedly doing nothing. At three thirty (while everyone upstairs washed their hands and lined up at the time clock), Carlton and Ken took off their gloves and laid them atop the half-emptied pallet. They walked through the packing room, where newly sealed tins of fish tumbled down chutes from the canning room above to be laid into cardboard boxes that were then stacked on pallets for shipping to supermarkets all over the U.S. and presumably the world. The packing crew had the best job in the place, as far as Carlton could tell—it was clean and simple and not physically demanding, and they were usually gone by two. Plus they got to take their breaks out on the dock by the harbor instead

65

of in the smoke-filled lunchroom or on the benches on the side of the building facing the parking lot.

But everyone was gone now, so the small sitting area at the top of the dock, with the spool table and a half dozen wooden chairs, was theirs alone. The two kids slouched against the wall of the building; Carlton, Ken, and the small supervisor took seats at the table. Everybody except Ken lit cigarettes. He and Carlton had paper cups from the coffee machine with poker hands on them. Ken's showed a pair of sevens; Carlton had an ace, king, jack, ten, and four. The hole card was on the bottom of the cup, and you couldn't see it until you finished most of the coffee. "Inside straight," Ken said, nodding at Carlton's cup. "I'll bet a quarter." He reached into his pocket and slapped a coin onto the table. They had played this game on every break today.

"These cups are rigged," Carlton said, and snickered. He matched Ken's bet and looked out at the harbor. It was a clear September day, which meant it was one of the finest days of the year on the Maine coast. The tide was coming in, about an hour away from high. A few boats motored around in the inner harbor, and several sails could be seen against the trees and cliffs of Harbor Island. Below their feet two empty fishing boats lay tied up at the dock. A seagull perched on the deck of one of them, and several more of the big, black-and-white birds circled lazily above.

All they needed, he thought, was a big fat doobie to pass around here on the dock. He'd been out of pot for nearly two weeks. And here was Steve, just back from New York with half a pound, on which he could make a small profit while smoking a fair amount of it himself. He knew Steve had to get rid of the dope, and hoped he wouldn't sell it to somebody else.

"Tell me something," Ken said. "Here's the ocean, right here, and here's two boats. . . . How come we're packing frozen fish that comes on a truck?"

Carlton shrugged and looked into his coffee. "Maybe they ain't catching enough. Maybe it's just business. Cheaper. Who knows?"

"They bring most of the fish into Prospect Harbor," the supervisor spoke up. "That or down to Bath. We don't hardly get any fish by boat. They truck it in."

Everybody thought this over in silence. Carlton took a drag on his cigarette and gazed back out at the water. Ken drank his coffee, looking through the inch of translucent murk at his hole card. "Raise you a quarter," he said.

Carlton sipped his coffee without looking at the bottom of his cup. He kept his face impassive. He reached into the pocket of his jeans. "What do you think of our Red Sox?" he asked.

Ken laughed. "That was one good thing about living in California," he said. "The Red Sox couldn't hurt me. At least not as much."

"This might be the year they do it," Carlton said. "They'll get the wild card, at least. And they still got a shot at the division title."

Ken drank the rest of his coffee and set down his cup. "They had a good weekend in New York, didn't they?" he said. "I'm glad they beat Clemens."

"How about that game Pedro pitched Friday night?" Carlton said. "One hit, seventeen strikeouts."

"He's amazing."

Carlton flipped a quarter onto the table. "Let's see what you got."

Ken slid his cup over to him. "Three sevens. What've you got?"

Carlton swallowed the last of his coffee, then tipped the cup so that Ken could see the card on the bottom. It was the queen of hearts.

Ken threw down his cup. "Luck," he said in disgust.

Carlton pocketed the four quarters.

"Strike three called," he said, standing up. The fifteen minutes were over. "Come on, let's get that fish unloaded so we can get the hell out of here."

FIVE

On a Thursday in late September, the first night of the full moon, Danny rowed his father to Harbor Island. But the scheme wasn't going to work in the long run. Winter was coming; there were bound to be days when it would be impossible to get there. And Liverpool was a small town. People would talk, and someone, sometime, would see them rowing out to the island and wonder why. All his father would say was, "It's better than San Diego."

Maybe for you, Danny thought. Sooner or later, something was sure to go wrong. It was difficult for Danny's father to make it to work on time even when he wasn't a werewolf.

He and Miranda suggested that Dad call in sick, but Friday was payday, and besides, he said, it was light at six in the morning. He made Danny promise to set his alarm, and they were back on shore by a quarter to seven. Ken was at the cannery only five minutes late.

Each day he came home at around four, his clothes covered with fish scales and exuding such an odor that Danny and Miranda checked the sky for hovering seagulls. He would shower, and place the clothes in a plastic bag in the bathroom for the next day's work. It had taken him one day to learn to wear his most ripped-up jeans and a shirt he didn't care if he ever saw again. He washed them once a week when the family went to the Laundromat, in a machine by themselves.

The house was roomier than any place they had lived in California. Danny and Miranda had the two downstairs bedrooms. Their father slept on the second floor, where the ceilings sloped inward and created triangular spaces. There was a backyard, and woods beyond that. Danny's friend Eric took to coming over after school and hanging out until five thirty or so, when his mother drove by to pick him up. Though she was a little bit overweight, Danny thought she was pretty in a frumpy sort of way he had come to associate with Maine. She had curly, reddish hair and took some care with her clothes. She was about his father's age. Her name was Beth.

They met one afternoon when Ken had got off work at the cannery, come home and showered, and was drinking a beer in his bathrobe in the living room. Danny cringed with embarrassment when his dad introduced himself.

"What, a man can't come home from a hard day's work and drink a cold beer in his own house?" his father said afterward.

"She's all dressed up and you're in your bathrobe."

"So?"

"So, it looks weird," Danny said lamely.

"Why?"

"I don't know. Forget it."

One afternoon he and Eric were playing Wiffle ball in the backyard when a car drove up, one of those dime-a-dozen American cars the kids in Maine drove, pale blue and rusted around the wheel wells. The driver, a scraggly-looking dude, leaned out the window and called Ken's name.

"Hey, Carlton," he heard his father say from the porch.

Ken went up to the car, and the two men spoke briefly. Dad went into the house and came out a minute later holding what looked like folded-up bills. He and Carlton exchanged something through the car window, and then Carlton gave him a hearty "See you later!" and drove off.

Well, it was pretty clear what had happened, and Danny's suspicions were confirmed a couple of hours later when Dad came in from an excursion into the woods behind the house with the unmistakable odor of weed on his breath. He had found a local dealer.

"My mom smokes pot," Eric told him the next day at school. "It makes her all stupid. Her boyfriend smokes too."

"I don't get what's so great about it," Danny said.

"I stole some from her once," Eric confided.

"She didn't even notice. Want me to try to get some?"

Danny shook his head. "My mom's an alcoholic," he said. "And my dad's a pothead. I don't see the sense in it."

"Me neither," Eric said. "Mom says half the people at AMIC are doing some kind of illegal drugs. She had to stop smoking for a couple months before she got the job, to pass their drug test."

Danny snorted. "Hey, you should come over at night sometime," he said. "I've got some fireworks."

After two weeks of lifting, throwing, carrying, and packing fish, Ken returned home, took an extralong shower, put on some cologne and clean clothes, and drove down to AMIC and asked for an application.

AMIC conducted a whole series of interviews before they hired someone. Most of the work was in the evening, because it consisted of calling people up at home and talking to them about their credit cards. After the fourth interview, they offered Ken a job, starting the following Monday. He had an appointment at the hospital on Thursday afternoon for his drug test.

Danny's first impulse was to refuse his father's strange request. "It's not my fault that you want to smoke that shit," he said. "You should have thought of it before."

"Come on, Danny, it'll mean a lot more money for all of us," his father said. "And it's an easy five bucks for you."

"Make it ten," Danny said.

"All right, you little capitalist, ten. Just do it, okay?"

It was against his principles, but Danny sold his father a jar of his urine for ten dollars, and his father took it to the hospital and passed his test. He quit at the packing plant the next day.

The next week Ken started orientation at AMIC. "Basically, it's just like selling magazine subscriptions, only they don't get a magazine."

"What *do* they get?" Danny asked.

"Nothing," his father said, and chuckled. "They get to borrow money. That's how AMIC's built their building and bought their land—by moving people's money around. I work for a billion-dollar company that produces nothing."

"At least you get to wear clean clothes," Miranda said.

Ken took them in during the first week of his employment, because there was a parent-teacher event at the high school immediately afterward, and because he wanted to show them where he worked. The lobby was carpeted and looked like it was vacuumed several times each day; the window glass bore not a trace of smudges or fingerprints. Their father had to sign them in and get them temporary badges, which they were required to wear in plain sight the whole time they were in the building. Danny thought it was spooky. You couldn't even get past the lobby without one of the electronic badges his father had, which activated the revolving door and set off a bunch of blinking lights. He almost preferred the stench and noise of the cannery.

On one wall of the lobby was a huge black-and-white picture of Liverpool Harbor in winter. From the quality of the photograph and the absence of modern buildings, Danny guessed the picture had been taken many years ago. The harbor was covered with ice. Huge sheets were stacked up against the rocks of Harbor Island, and a group of bearded men and several horses stood on what was now open water.

"Check this out," Danny said. Miranda and his father moved over for a closer look.

"I didn't think the harbor ever froze over like that," Ken said.

The old man in the glassed-in security booth had been watching them over the rims of his glasses.

"That picture used to be in the old county administration building, before they tore it down," he said. "The newspaper had it blown up for the state sesquicentennial. It hung there for many years, until AMIC bought it."

"I see," their father said.

"Used to be a lot colder in the winters than it is now," the old man said. "Used to freeze over every year, back when I was a boy. No more."

"You could walk on the ice?" Danny said. "All the way to the island?"

"Oh, ayuh. They used to drag wood off'n that island with horses. Couldn't do it today. I gotta think there's something to that global warming they keep talking about."

"When was this picture taken?" Ken asked him.

"Oh, it was backalong," the old man said. "Bay don't freeze like that no more. Hasn't frozen over for some fifty years."

"Well, that's good to know," Ken said. Danny looked at his father, and then at his sister, and knew what they were thinking.

One evening a few days later their father came home from work happy and humming to himself, and finally Miranda asked him what was going on. He had met a young woman at AMIC, he said. "She's an actress," he told them. "She's got a part in some play at the community theater. They need someone to do a walk-on. I might do it."

"Dad, be serious," Miranda said.

"I am being serious. I did some acting in high school. And there're only three lines. Besides, it'd be a way to meet some people outside of work."

"We could've just stayed in California."

"You know why we couldn't have stayed in California," Ken said.

"Why? Because you're a werewolf? Well, here we are in Maine, and guess what? You're still a werewolf."

"There're fewer people in Maine. And there's Harbor Island."

"I thought you wanted to keep a low profile," Miranda retorted. "Now you want to go onstage in front of the whole town? What're you going to do if one of the performances is on a full moon?"

"I already checked the dates," their father said. "I'll be fine."

Her name was Michelle, and over the next few days their father drove Danny and Miranda nuts by singing that dumb Beatles song and playing it on the stereo. "The Beatles and *Star Trek*," Miranda griped to her brother, out of their father's hearing. "He lives in a time warp."

Ken dragged Danny and Miranda to his first rehearsal so that they could see the theater, which was down by the waterfront, about half a mile up from AMIC. The funky, wooden, brick-red building had once been a railroad depot; extra props and stage materials were kept in an actual freight car out back. A massive wood porch, grayed by the weather, surrounded the building on three sides. The rails in back, between the theater and the harbor, had long ago been abandoned. But the building remained an organic part of its surroundings. There was a boatyard next door, and the docks of the fish cannery on the other side. AMIC had removed all vestiges of the old working waterfront from its property, except for a large mushroom anchor that stood near the entrance as a kind of trophy. They had built a park and put in benches of new wood and wrought iron, and it was a comfortable place to take a stroll or a lunch break on a sunny day. Still, it didn't fit in. There was a line between AMIC and non-AMIC real estate, and though it was not painted on the land, you could feel it when you crossed it. The air itself changed.

The theater was like an old barn inside—the walls were dark wood and the seats were old church pews. It was cold in there, because they turned off the heater during rehearsal so the blower wouldn't interfere with the actors saying their lines. Ken had to fire a rifle in his one scene, and Danny was embarrassed for him because another actor had to show him how. Danny's father was antiguns—he had never allowed Danny to have a toy gun when he was younger—and he didn't know how to hold the thing properly.

Miranda disliked Michelle immediately. "You see how the major male characters fight over her," she said to her father afterward. "I'll bet she's like that in real life. Has to be the center of attention all the time."

"She's got my attention," Dad said. "She's just my type, too—dark hair and blue eyes, like your mom."

"What makes you think she's even interested in you, Dad?" Miranda said. "She's a little young, don't you think?"

"She's twenty-eight," Dad said. "Ten thousand days. It's a the perfect age for a woman."

"And you're forty-two and going gray."

"So what? Lots of women hook up with older men."

"Yeah, but usually the men are rich, and tall, and handsome."

"I'll be rich after I get my screenplay sold."

"Dream on, Dad," Miranda said. "Besides, she's not even that pretty."

"You don't think so? I do."

"Well, maybe for Maine," Miranda said. "In California nobody would give her a second glance."

"Yeah they would. And she's not even from here. She's from New York. She just moved here. We have that in common, at least."

"Have you told her you're a werewolf?"

"I thought I'd wait until we got to know each other a little better."

"Oh, right." Miranda rolled her eyes. "I can just imagine what she'll say."

"She'll think you're crazy, Dad," Danny told him.

He and his sister exchanged a wary look. They had problems of their own, trying to fit into Liverpool. Danny's friend Eric was sweet on Miranda, which was demeaning to her because Eric was only a freshman (though he had stayed back a year somewhere along the line). Danny had half a dozen freshman girls calling him up periodically and giggling. What did he care about his father's love life? Why did Dad always have to complicate things? The werewolf business was bad enough by itself.

"Look, I'm not just going to go curl up in a cave somewhere and die."

Obviously Danny's father had decided that the time was right for a midlife crisis, and nothing Danny or Miranda could say would discourage him. All of a sudden their father began paying attention to his thinning hair, shaving every day instead of every other, and wearing cologne. He didn't have to go to many rehearsals, since his part was small, but sometimes he went anyway.

The days were growing shorter, darker, and colder. The school bus had its headlights on in the predawn glow when it stopped across the street to pick them up. During the week Danny and Miranda saw little of their father. On weekends they often took short car trips along the Maine coast and into the countryside. Dad wanted to show them where he had grown up. They visited their grandparents, farther up the coast, and one weekend they drove all the way to Lubec. They stopped at yard sales and bought stuff for the house. Miranda remarked that it was hard to tell in Maine whether a house was having a yard sale or just had a lot of junk lying around. But they got a wooden table and a set of chairs for the kitchen in this manner, though one of the chairs had a crack in it and the table needed refinishing.

September passed into October, and a few nights later a thin crescent moon appeared in the evening over the trees behind the house. None of them had to say aloud what it meant. The time was coming around again. And nothing in the universe could stop it.

SIX

October was the month of the baseball playoffs, and
Danny's father paid attention to baseball. The previous season Danny had paid attention too, because the Padres had won the National League pennant and made it to the World Series. His dad had rooted for the Padres in San Diego, but this year the Red Sox had made the playoffs, and it was, as the announcers on TV said, a whole different ball game.

Ken couldn't sit still. The Red Sox won the division series against Cleveland in a winner-take-all fifth game. Ken got several phone calls that night from friends in different parts of the country.

The score was 8–8 in the fourth inning, and then Pedro Martinez, who'd been hurt and wasn't supposed to pitch, came in and held the Indians hitless for the rest of the game. Danny's father stomped around the house, proclaiming, "This is the year! You watch—this is the year!"

But the Red Sox had to play the Yankees in the next series. Danny knew all about the Yankees, whom his father seldom talked about without appending an expletive to their name. Danny had never cared about baseball the way his father did, though he had played Little League in San Diego and attended a handful of Padres games. His dad's first date with his disastrous post-Mom girlfriend had been a baseball game with Danny and Miranda and one of Miranda's friends. The Padres were terrible that year, and there were about a hundred people in the stadium. Dad had paid for cheap seats and then moved them all into the expensive section, close to the action. Fernando Valenzuela pitched for the Padres, and the small crowd was made up mostly of Mexicans. And Fernando, who looked too fat to run to first base and whose fastball, by that point in his career, wasn't much, not only won the game, but hit a home run besides.

He had heard his father talk about the Red Sox as he read the morning paper. He knew they hadn't won the World Series in a long, long time. He knew that the Yankees always ate the Red Sox's lunch when it counted, and that there was no way the Red Sox were going to win this time either.

But you couldn't tell that to his father. "The better team doesn't always win," he insisted. "In seventy-eight the Red Sox were better, and the Yankees beat 'em anyway. This year it's our turn." And so on.

Danny's father watched the games. But he didn't just watch them. He had to sit in his lucky chair, and he debated aloud whether or not to wear his Red Sox cap, whether it would bring them good luck or jinx them. Danny and Miranda laughed. "You don't understand," he said. "The portents have to be right."

The Yankees won the first game of the series in ten innings. Danny wasn't around to see it, because the game ended after midnight. It hadn't started until almost nine, which his father declared was ridiculous.

"They should play these games during the day," he said. "It's October, for Christ's sake—it's about twenty degrees out. When I was a kid, all World Series games were played during the day, even in the middle of the week. You'd pass people on the street or in the school corridor and ask what the score was. It brought the whole country together."

"Times have changed, Dad," Miranda said.

"Yeah, and not for the better. The greatest team sport ever invented is now enslaved by the boob tube. Television dictates the schedule, so they can raise more advertising revenue so they can pay the players more. They play the World Series entirely at night so it won't conflict with the football schedule. And a whole generation of kids is growing up without the shared experience of the World Series."

"It's just baseball, Dad," Danny said.

"Corporate baseball," he shot back. "It stinks. It's another example of the corporate world taking something grand, something with soul, and destroying it through mass merchandising."

Here he goes again, Danny and Miranda said to each other with their eyes. They were all too familiar with this rant. He'd change the channel on TV whenever a commercial came on. "Advertising," he'd mumble in disgust.

"How are they supposed to sell their stuff if they don't advertise?" Miranda asked him.

"By making good products," Ken said. "You only see huge advertising budgets when there's no difference between them. Like McDonald's and Burger King. Or Budweiser and Coors. If you were blindfolded, could you tell the difference between Budweiser and Coors?"

"I don't know. I don't drink beer."

"They put a bunch of horses, or girls in bathing suits, or clear Rocky Mountain streams on TV, and try to build brand loyalty," Dad said. "McDonald's advertises with litter. You see their logo enough times on roadside trash, pretty soon you're convinced you gotta have a Big Mac or an Egg McMuffin."

"I like Egg McMuffins," Danny said.

"You're a victim of corporate brainwashing," his father told him.

"Face it, Dad, that's the way the world is,"

Miranda said. "Personally, I'd rather shop at Wal-Mart than those dinky stores on Main Street. Wal-Mart has everything you need, and the prices are lower."

"And pretty soon the little stores that can't compete will go out of business, and the family that once ran its own store will have to go to work for the big corporation."

"So? What's wrong with that?"

"Pretty soon Maine's gonna look just like Indiana. It's already started. Look at this little town. In another ten years it's gonna be owned and operated by the AMIC corporation."

"Which you work for," Danny reminded him.

"Dad, corporations rule the world," Miranda said. "It's just like what you say when you tell Danny and me what to do and we argue. 'I pay the rent around here.' They've got the power. That's just the way it is."

"Yeah, Dad," Danny put in. "You're always power tripping on us. Why shouldn't the corporate world power trip on *you*?"

"You're just mad because you're not in charge," Miranda said.

Danny could see his father starting to smile in spite of himself. "Yeah, well, when I become president, the corporate world better tremble in its boots," he mumbled.

His father had figured out that if the series went seven games, he'd have to miss the finale, because the game would be played on the first night of the full moon. He said he didn't mind, because in the event of a seventh, deciding game between the Red Sox and the Yankees, he would be so riddled with anxiety that he might turn into a werewolf spontaneously, without the help of the Moon.

Danny didn't know whether that was possible, but it began to look more likely than the Red Sox extending the series to its limit. They did manage to win one game, a 13–1 blowout at Fenway Park on a sunny Saturday afternoon. At first Ken was excited, but then he began to fret that the Red Sox were wasting all their runs on this one game.

The Red Sox lost the series in five. The other games were close, and the Yankees benefitted from a couple of dubious calls, which the TV cameras showed over and over from every possible angle while Ken screamed at the television. And on the evening of what would have been the seventh game, while the Yankees rested up for the World Series, Danny rowed his father out to Harbor Island.

"Maybe in *your* lifetime they'll win it," his father murmured as he slumped in the stern, dragging his fingers through the cold, calm water.

"Dad, I don't much care," Danny said.

"You don't understand," his father said. "My grandfather, who's twenty years dead, was a foot soldier in World War One the last time the Red Sox won the World Series. My father hadn't even been born yet. Generations of Red Sox fans have lived, worked, had children, and died without seeing a championship. In a way, it's like being a werewolf. Maybe when a Red Sox fan dies, he or she has to remain in purgatory until they finally win it all."

"If so," Danny replied, pulling on the oars, "purgatory must be getting awfully crowded."

"Smart-ass kid," Ken mumbled. But the corners of his mouth turned upward, and Danny took that as a good sign. Like most romantics, his father was an eternal optimist. He always held on to the possibility of a ninth-inning rally. Baseball, he'd say, was a metaphor for life in a way that other sports could never be. He would point out that a team could come back from twenty runs down as long as it didn't make three outs. Other sports had clocks that could be run out. Not baseball. Hope never died on a baseball diamond, he said. Nor should it die in life.

Ken had constructed a rudimentary shelter on Harbor Island in the ruins of the old foundation. He'd dug a hole into the side of what had once been the wall of the basement, and hollowed out a space several times bigger than himself. This he'd lined with spruce boughs along the floor and sides, so that it was actually pretty cozy. *An animal's den,* Danny thought with a shudder. But it would be warm, even in winter.

This was a Thursday night. His father had told the people at AMIC he had an appointment in New York with an agent who was interested in his screenplay—a total lie, but one that got him out of work for the evening. AMIC didn't call customers on Friday or Saturday nights, but they did run day shifts on Saturdays, and the deal was that you had to work two Saturdays a month. Ken had to work the next two shifts, from nine in the morning to one in the afternoon. Danny wanted to stay and camp out on the south end of Harbor Island, bringing a bunch of silver stuff to scatter around the tent, but Dad strongly vetoed the idea. So Danny had to row out again and get him first thing the next morning. And the mornings were getting cold!

There was a little bit of wind that Friday morning. The oars kept hitting the tops of the waves and splashing Danny with cold water as he rowed. A lobster boat headed out from the harbor toward the open ocean against the red sky. The guy at the wheel saw him and changed course.

"You need any help?" he called out when he came up alongside. He had on tall rubber boots and a bright orange slicker that he wore like an apron. He was alone on the boat, standing at the wheelhouse. The whole back of the boat was empty except for several plastic buckets. Danny could smell baitfish, and so could the seagulls that hovered in a cloud above him, squawking and whirling. Danny hoped they wouldn't leave a calling card. He shook his head and kept rowing.

"You sure?"

"Sure I'm sure," he said, trying not to sound irritated. "I'm just getting some exercise."

"Kinda rough out heah." The lobsterman looked at Danny for a long time, not saying anything. He didn't seem to be in any hurry to get to his lobster traps.

Danny stopped rowing and held the oars flat, a couple of inches above the wave tops. "I'm all right," he said.

They were halfway between the island and the shore. The lobsterman could plainly see the two life jackets Danny had in the boat, and the knapsack full of clean, warm clothes for his father. He must have known Danny was headed for the island, and he must have wondered why. But he didn't say anything. Finally he sort of shrugged and kicked the engine into gear. "You be careful," was the last thing he said, and then he headed out into the bay.

Danny waited a few minutes before he resumed rowing. His mind churned with worry. He watched the twin lines of the lobster boat's wake diverge as the boat itself grew smaller against the sky. The Sun came up, fuzzed by red morning clouds. Dad was waiting on the shore for him, huddled in the parka they'd stashed in a tree the night before. His face was pinched and gaunt, and his eyes were bloodshot.

"Dad, we may have a problem," Danny said.

SEVEN

"Son of a bitch," Carlton Reynolds said to himself when he heard the news. "They're gonna discover my crop."

He'd been meaning to get out to the island anyway, because it was late in the season and the nights were getting cold. Not that frost would hurt his plants too much, but they *were* illegal, and he couldn't very well harvest them in daylight. They were weeds; they stood up to anything. You just put the seeds in the ground, hit 'em with water and Miracle-Gro a few times when they were young, and let the Sun do the rest. The biggest danger was discovery by human beings. He'd had friends who'd started seedlings indoors in March, carefully transplanted them in May and nurtured them all through the summer, only to have the whole harvest uprooted by thieves in September. And what could you do about it? Even if the plants were on your own land, you couldn't very well go to the police.

And that was how he had hit on the brilliant idea of planting his crop on Harbor Island.

He'd found a spot near the island's far shore, the side facing away from town, where the trees thinned out a bit and offered limited exposure to the south. His cousin Seth had sold him a small boat with an outboard motor, and during the spring and summer Carlton had made several trips to the island, always bringing a bucket and a clam fork or a fishing rod in case anybody asked any questions. Nobody did. Nobody went out to the island except a few occasional kayakers, and they seemed to stick to the shore. Carlton had carved a small path to his patch of cultivated land, but it was a path you wouldn't see unless you were looking for it, marked by diagonal slashes on the trees that could have been mistaken for the signs of an animal sharpening its claws. Not that there were a lot of animals with claws on the island, though Carlton had seen evidence of deer and porcupine, and the possibility of fox or bobcat or even a bear or two could not be completely ruled out.

Sometimes he'd come across a spent shotgun shell or a rusting can, one of those old beer cans with the pull-off tabs that were now against the law. But the people of Liverpool had turned their backs on Harbor Island when they could no longer go out there to hunt and build campfires and throw their empties into the woods. He'd heard family members curse the goddamned government for taking the island away from them, but secretly he was glad. It meant that no one would be likely to interfere with his business.

But now Seth had seen some kid rowing out to the island in the early morning. And Carlton was worried.

He should have harvested the crop weeks ago. He'd been dithering about it since mid-September, when he'd come back from the island with his pockets filled with buds from the tops of his two best plants, which were taller than he was. But the stuff he'd been getting from Steve was more than adequate, and he didn't want to arouse suspicion. He had told no one about his crop. He made a little bit of profit off the stuff he got from Steve, but the plants on the island would see him through the winter with plenty to spare. First, however, he had to get it off the island without being seen. And that presented a problem. The plants would fill at least two garbage bags. He couldn't very well bring them ashore in full view of the town. It had to be done at night. It had to be done, in fact, this weekend, when the full moon would light his way. The harvest moon. It was perfect, as long as no one interfered.

But what had that kid been doing out there? Probably some brat whose parents worked for AMIC and had bought him a rowboat for his birthday. Well, that birthday present could easily end up at the bottom of the bay. It was a simple matter of drilling a few well-placed holes.

Carlton hoped it wouldn't come to that. But he

100

was worried as he made his preparations after work to go out to the island. In his mind he saw his summer's work decimated, and a bunch of fourteen-year-olds getting stoned behind the gym before school on the fruits of *his* labor. He hoped he wouldn't arrive at his secret spot to find all his plants uprooted or chopped down, but he feared he would find exactly that.

He packed a heavy sweater and a windbreaker, a box of heavy-duty garbage bags, a peanut-butter-and-jelly sandwich and a box of chocolate-covered granola bars, a machete with a foot-long blade to cut the plants with, a flashlight, and a pistol, just in case. He decided to take his fishing rod and tackle box for cover, though it would seem implausible that anyone would go fishing in Liverpool Harbor in the middle of the night. He kept his boat down at Seth's dock on the eastern side of the harbor. Seth's family went to bed early, because he got up before dawn to go haul his lobsters. Carlton had worked with Seth for a while as a stern man, but he'd hated getting up at four in the morning. And spending the day out on the water, stuffing bait bags and cleaning algae off buoy lines, wasn't his idea of a good time. His current job, at the fish factory, was really just for cover. There was more money to be made dealing dope, and the hours were better.

He waited until the lights went off in his cousin's house, and then he waited an hour after that. He untied the boat from the dock and let it drift silently out into the harbor. It was a nice night—cold, but the wind had died down, and the Moon cast a yellow glow over everything. More than half the boats that had been moored in the harbor over the summer were gone. There had been a lot more working boats in the harbor when Carlton was a boy, but now Liverpool was home mainly to expensive sailboats, which seemed to show up on their moorings in June and, with rare exceptions, to seldom leave them until they disappeared again at the beginning of September. Carlton couldn't understand how someone could own a hundred thousand dollars' worth of boat and use it once or twice a year. Seth was the only person he knew who worked the ocean and still lived on the shore, close to the water. There were a couple of other working lobster boats in the harbor, but their owners lived inland on modest parcels of land and had to drive to the harbor.

He drifted outward on the tide, occasionally dipping the oars into the water to help the boat along. He watched two trucks rumble across the high bridge over the inner harbor. A single spotlight shone from the roof of the fish plant, and the lights of the town landing were reflected in the water. The lone traffic light blinked like a yellow lighthouse; after nine o'clock it no longer stopped traffic but merely admonished it to slow down. Farther along the shore, the AMIC corporation blazed more brightly than the town itself, more brightly than the Moon.

Carlton waited until he was well away from Seth's dock before he started the engine. The black bulk of Harbor Island loomed in front of him at the harbor's mouth. It comforted him that there were no lights among the trees. At least one chunk of land in Liverpool would remain the way it was, forever.

He motored slowly in the direction of the open ocean and exhaled with relief when the bulk of the island interposed itself between the boat and the lights of AMIC. He moved in close to the shore and slowed the engine further, staying outside the rocks that at midtide would be looming just underneath the water's surface. Moonlight made the shoreline easy to follow. He reached into his knapsack and pulled out the box of granola bars. He unwrapped one and chewed it slowly. The sugar would help him keep warm. When he spotted the boulder on the shore that marked his landing spot, he pointed the boat toward it and cut the engine. He polished off the granola bar and put the wrapper in the pocket of his sweatshirt, tilted the motor up out of the water, and paddled the boat in toward shore with one oar, like a Louisiana riverboat. The boat crunched against the gravel bottom and came to rest.

He looked at his watch. Ten minutes to eleven. The tide would be low at midnight, which meant he could leave the boat where it was and have two hours to harvest the plants before it floated again. Plenty of time. Nonetheless, he found a pillow-size rock and secured the painter to it. The whole shore was bathed in moonlight. He didn't need to use his flashlight. It would be darker in the woods, but he was confident he could find his way. He pulled on his sweater, ate another granola bar, shouldered his knapsack, and grabbed the machete from the bottom of the boat. He looked back at the water and saw nothing. No one had seen him, apparently, and that was good.

He walked down the shore toward the large spruce tree whose roots lay half exposed at the top of the bank. Behind this tree was another tree, similar in size but firmly embedded in the soil of the island. By lining up these two trees, Carlton would be able to find a birch tree with a diagonal slash through the bark at eye level, and he could then follow similar slashes until he came to the small open area where he had planted his seeds last May.

The moonlight cast weird shadows through the trees. Carlton stopped at the first slash mark and listened. There was no wind, but he thought he'd heard a rustling noise in the woods in front of him. Maybe his footsteps had spooked a sleeping animal. He took a few cautious steps forward, then stopped to listen again. This time he thought he heard a low growl. The hair on the back of his neck prickled. He took off his backpack and felt around inside it for his flashlight.

A flock of birds burst from the trees in front of him. Carlton stepped back, startled, and dropped his pack on the ground. A crow cawed once, and suddenly the sky was alive with birds. Carlton could see them against the Moon. The light around him flickered. He became aware of his heart, thumping against the inside of his chest.

And then he heard another sound—not of birds, but of an animal in severe distress. Mortal distress, quite likely—there was the growl again, but barely noticeable against the thrashing in the underbrush and the *screams*—that was all he would be able to think to call them, when he started to think again—of something dying violently. "Jesus Christ," he said aloud, before he could stop himself.

The screams stopped as quickly as they had started, but Carlton could still hear the undersounds—the thrashing and growling and, farther off, the beating of wings in the cold night air. His mouth was suddenly dry. What was going on? He retrieved the pack, and with trembling hands managed to extract the flashlight and turn it on. He stabbed the beam into the trees in front of him. There was the next slash mark, across the trunk of an emaciated little spruce tree squarely in the direction from which the sounds were coming. He tried to swallow but produced only a painful click. Gripping the flashlight in one hand and the machete in the other, he crept slowly forward.

Something was feeding in the clearing. As he drew closer, Carlton could hear the sounds of animal savagery. His flashlight beam picked out the next slash mark, and the next. . . .

And suddenly the sounds stopped. The animal had sensed his presence. It could smell him, Carlton surmised, just as he could smell the warm blood of the creature it had killed. All at once his crop didn't matter so much. What mattered was getting out of there alive.

He turned off the flashlight. Slowly, making as little noise as possible, he began to retrace his steps back toward the shore, toward the safety of his boat. He was shaking all over.

It was dead quiet again. Carlton imagined he could hear his own heart pounding. What the hell was out here with him—a bear, a lynx, some sort of feral dog? Whatever it was, Carlton had the distinct impression it was stalking him.

Several small trees had blown down across the path Carlton had marked, and he hadn't bothered to remove them, for their presence made it look less like a path. He had stepped over them easily on the way in; the Moon provided plenty of light for him to watch his footing. But now in his eagerness to be somewhere—anywhere—else, he caught his foot on one of the blowdowns and stumbled to the forest floor. The machete fell from his hand. Desperately he reached around for it.

And there was that low growling again, much closer! Carlton got to his feet, forgetting the knife. He flipped on the flashlight. Something was definitely moving in the trees behind him. He didn't want to wait for a good look at it. He turned and ran.

He reached the shore in seconds, leaping from

the top of the bank over the roots of the big spruce tree, landing in a crouch on the shells and seaweed. There was the boat, a short sprint away, high and dry in the moonlight. And there were crashing noises in the woods above him, as the animal closed in pursuit. He ran for the boat.

The tide had receded from beneath the boat's stern. Carlton stripped off the pack, threw it into the boat, put his shoulder to the bow and pushed. The boat didn't budge. Panicked, he leaned his weight into it again, with the same result. *The line!* Quickly he freed it from the rock and pushed again. This time the boat began to slide over the mud and gravel. *Yes!*

A tree limb snapped with a sound like a gunshot. Carlton looked up at the big spruce. A black animal shape, yellow eyes gleaming in the moonlight, stepped out onto the bank. It was huge— easily the size of a man. "Come on, come on!" Carlton cried between his teeth as he pushed the boat toward the water. With a roar, the creature leaped from the bank and bounded toward him.

Carlton remembered the pistol. His feet in the

water now, he reached into the boat, grabbed the pack, unzipped it, and rummaged around inside until he felt the gun. The creature was coming for him, on all fours at a dead run. Carlton swung the pistol around and fired. The bullet pinged off a rock. The thing kept coming for him. Carlton steadied the gun with both hands and fired again.

Son of a bitch! The creature roared in fury, fell to the ground, and got up again! Carlton couldn't believe it. He had hit it right between the eyes! He fired again, hitting it just below the neck. The animal stopped, looked at itself, and then at Carlton again. "Die, you fucker!" Carlton screamed, and fired two more shots. The thing staggered but did not fall. Carlton threw the pack and the gun into the boat and pushed with all his remaining strength. And—thanks be to God!—the boat floated. He jumped in, grabbed an oar, and pushed off just as his pursuer reached the edge of the water.

And then, to Carlton's horrified disbelief, the thing stood up on its hind legs and waded in after him! Carlton swung the oar and cracked it on the side of the head. The animal staggered backward, but only momentarily. Growling low in its throat, it came after him again. Carlton hit it again with the oar. This time the animal roared and swiped the oar out of his hands. Carlton could see its mouth, filled with sharp, canine teeth. He could smell its breath. It stank like nothing he had ever smelled before. The creature reeked of blood, of death, and of something rotten, something so hideous that Carlton had no association for it. As though it had been feasting on rotted corpses.

He had only one chance: the motor. He prayed there was enough water under the boat for the propeller to turn. He slammed the motor down, opened the choke, and yanked the cord. The motor sputtered and died. "Come on! Come on! Sweet Jesus, *come on!*" He yanked the cord again, and this time the engine started. The creature swiped a furry paw at him and laid open the skin on his forearm. Carlton slammed the engine into forward and pointed the boat away from shore. He knew the tide was out and there were rocks, but he was relying on blind luck now. He felt the boat jerk away from the grasp of the creature. The thing roared one more time, and Carlton thought crazily that it meant to swim after him. The boat careened toward open water. Carlton looked back and saw the animal retreat onto the shore, drop to all fours, and bound back up into the trees.

Carlton was halfway across the channel between the island and the shore before he noticed that his arm was bleeding. The animal's claws had cut right through his sweater and shirt and into his flesh. He stopped the engine and let the boat drift in the moonlight, and he dipped his arm in the cold water. He exhaled slowly, trying to calm his racing heart. After a minute he yanked his arm out of the water. What was he trying to do, call sharks? He laughed nervously. He'd heard all his life that the water in Maine was too cold for the kinds of sharks that attacked humans, but after what he had just seen, he wasn't inclined to trust the vagaries of nature.

What *had* he seen? What kind of animal had attacked him, and kept attacking him even after being struck by at least three bullets? It wasn't a bear—he was all but certain of that. Had someone discovered his plants and left some kind of superbred attack dog to guard them? But the thing had stood on its hind legs and used its forelegs as arms. And nothing seemed to stop it. What *was* it, anyway?

He looked at his arm. It was really bleeding badly. He would need to bandage it soon. But first he needed to get to shore without being noticed. Surely someone in town had heard the shots. And the pistol lay in the bottom of the boat. He reached down with his good arm and stuffed it back in the pack. Then he pulled off his sweater, pulled off his sweatshirt, wrapped the sweatshirt around the wound and put the sweater back on over his shoulders and his good arm. He looked around the moonlit bay. Nothing. Well, he sure as hell wasn't going to paddle back to shore with one oar and one arm. He started the engine.

He motored at low speed toward the nearest point on land. As he approached he had another thought. Everything in the boat was covered with blood. Shouldn't he throw the pistol overboard, in case someone saw him and connected him to the shots on the island? What if someone investigated and discovered his plants? And how was he supposed to go back and harvest them, with that . . . *thing* out there?

He took the pistol out and was on the verge of throwing it over the side when the bottom of the boat bumped against something solid. He cut the engine and laid the gun on top of the bloody knapsack. He was close to shore now. The lights in the nearby houses were out. Half of them belonged to summer people who were gone by this time in the fall. He took out the remaining oar and began poling himself along the bottom toward his cousin's dock.

It took a while, but he didn't want to risk the engine again. Seth's lobster boat was tied up at the dock. Carlton went aboard and found a big sponge. He spent the next hour washing every trace of blood from his boat. The Moon was low over the town by the time he finished and crept off into the night, toward his car. If he could just get home without being seen, everything would be all right. He'd wash out the wound on his arm and dress it, and then he'd go to sleep, and when he woke up, maybe the whole night's adventure would turn out to have been simply a bad dream.

EIGHT

Danny waited until the lobster boat had gone out into the bay before he rowed to the island. He could see his breath, and cold, wispy mist rose from the calm surface of the water. A pair of thick gloves kept his hands warm while he rowed and helped with the blisters, too. It had only taken him two months to figure this out, but then, what did he know? He was a California kid in a foreign country.

His father wasn't on the shore when Danny landed, and he felt a prickle of worry. Usually Dad was right there waiting for the boat. A cloud of birds, like the flocks that followed the fishing boats, hovered over the other end of the island, but Danny didn't give them much thought. The tide was up. He secured the painter to a tree root and went to look for his father.

He wasn't at the old foundation. Danny looked inside the cave he'd made for himself and saw the boughs he'd lined it with, the old blankets they had brought out, the small bag that contained a flashlight, an emergency hand warmer and a change of clothes, the cooler in which his father always kept a few cans of beer. His shoes were laid neatly, one beside the other, next to the cooler. Everything was still there. It looked like he hadn't used the shelter at all.

In the distance Danny thought he heard the buzz of a small outboard motor, but he couldn't be sure. The Sun poked through the trees but did not yet offer much warmth. Danny climbed up out of the ruined foundation and saw his father approaching him from the other side of the clearing.

He looked awful. His shirt was in tatters—just strips of fabric hanging from its collar. His pants were torn at the knees. He was barefoot, of course—he had told Danny and Miranda that he purposefully took off his shoes before the transformation, because while pants and shirts could be easily replaced, he couldn't afford to buy a new pair of shoes every month. He had cut himself in several places, including a deep gouge right above his eyes. The blood had dried incompletely, and he had wiped at it, leaving a dark red stain across one whole side of his face. There were other scratches on his torso, and his feet were cut and filthy, as if he had walked through mud. Parts of the forest clung to him—twigs in his hair, a piece of moss sticking out of a hole in his jeans, some sort of sap spread along a nasty scrape near his rib cage. He staggered toward his son. Danny ran to him and helped him sit down at the edge of the foundation.

"Dad! Are you all right?"

His father smiled crookedly. "Do I look all right? Do me a favor—get me one of those beers out of the cooler. Oh, man, do I have a headache."

Reluctantly Danny got him a beer. His father drained half the can in one gulp.

"What happened?" Danny asked him.

His father took a more moderate pull from the

can. "Whaddya mean, what happened? I'm a werewolf. I don't remember what happens."

"Yeah, but you're never in *this* bad shape. We gotta get you cleaned up and back to the mainland. You're gonna be late for work."

"Forget work. You're going to have to call me in sick. Get me my clothes, will ya?"

Ken finished the beer and groaned as he tried to get up. "Stay where you are," Danny said. "I'll get 'em." He held out his hand for the empty can. His father was a stickler about littering, and he always made sure he cleaned up after himself. His hideout on Harbor Island reflected his fastidiousness. Outside his little cave you couldn't tell that he'd ever been there.

Danny helped him clean up. They took everything but the blankets, which they folded neatly and laid at the back of the cave. The full moon was over; his father wouldn't be returning until November. At the shore Ken took off his ruined clothes and plunged into the frigid water.

He approached the cold Maine water the same way every time. He never waded in; instead, he got up a running start and immersed himself all at once. He swam half a dozen strokes before his body woke up to the fact of how cold the water was. This ritual was usually accompanied by some sort of banshee yell. Then he'd stand up, gasping, in chest-deep water, and call out in a constricted voice, "Hey! It's not too bad!"

But today he stayed in the water for several minutes, rubbing off the blood and dirt with his hands. When he finally came out, Danny couldn't help but notice the angry red pockmarks on his chest, like someone had jabbed him several times with a sharp stick. That's what the cut on his forehead looked like too, once he'd wiped away the dried blood. Danny could tell he was sore as he dried himself off and put on his clean clothes. On the long row back to the mainland, he slumped in the stern, not saying much, one hand draped loosely over the side of the boat, the other wrapped around the second beer of the day. It wasn't even eight o'clock yet.

Danny called AMIC and talked to a receptionist, who said she'd notify his father's supervisor that he would not be in that day. Ken went to sleep for several hours, and since it was Saturday, Danny made himself four pieces of cinnamon toast and settled in to watch cartoons.

Miranda got up around noon, and Dad emerged an hour or so later and went to take a shower. When he came out, with a towel wrapped around his waist, Danny noticed that the cuts on his chest and forehead were already fading. *Werewolves heal fast,* he thought. And a good thing, too—otherwise they'd never be able to live normal lives between full moons. They'd walk around all scarred and cut up, and everyone would know what they were. Which, Danny reflected, might make the world a safer place.

Ken put on a Beatles record and made a huge breakfast of eggs and hash brown potatoes, even though it was two in the afternoon. He was in a good mood. He always seemed to be in a good mood after the end of the full moon.

That night they ordered pizza and watched the opening game of the World Series, and Ken didn't even get upset when the Yankees won. They were playing the Braves, and he said he really didn't care about the outcome, but that he always rooted for the National League team unless the Red Sox were in the Series, because he hated the designated hitter. "Besides, the Yankees have won enough championships. Everybody outside of New York is sick of them."

But on Sunday things began to unravel. First their mother called from California. She was three sheets to the wind and had had a fight with her boyfriend, and was thinking about coming out to Maine to be closer to her children. This made Ken predictably nervous, and he went into the back-yard and smoked a joint. It wasn't fifteen minutes later that a police car pulled into the driveway and two uniformed officers got out and walked up to the front porch.

Dad saw them coming and told Miranda to answer the door while he went into the bathroom and brushed his teeth. The cops asked if their father was home, and Miranda said yes, he was in the bath-room and would be right out. "Is he in trouble?" Miranda asked. She kept the screen door closed.

"We just want to ask him a few questions," said the cop closest to the door, avoiding a direct answer to her question. He was big and blond, his hair shaved close in back and all around the sides and push-broom-bristle-length on top. He looked like he had been a football player in high school but had spent the years since then indulging his fondness for doughnuts. His partner was shorter and thinner, with dark hair slicked to his scalp on either side of a ruler-straight part. Danny hung back in the corner of the living room, close enough to hear what was said without being seen.

"I'll go get him," Miranda said, all business. "Wait here." One of the things Danny admired about his sister was that she wasn't intimidated by anyone, not even police officers in uniform on her front porch.

Dad came out of the bathroom before she could knock. "What can I do for you guys?" he asked the cops in a voice that was so friendly it had to arouse their immediate suspicion. Nobody—not even the most upstanding, church-going, DARE program-supporting pillar of the community—is happy to see two policeman in uniform show up at the front door. Their father sounded like he was about to invite them in for beers and hot dogs. Danny thought about the arsenal of fireworks in his bedroom.

"Mr. Paxton?" said the first officer.

"That's me," Ken replied. Danny could tell that he was nervous, but he kept trying to hide it by an exaggerated show of friendliness.

"We'd like to ask you a couple of questions, if we could."

"About what?"

"It'll only take a few minutes. You mind if we come in?"

On the porch was a spool table their father had bought at a yard sale for two bucks, and four plastic chairs he'd found at the dump. "We can talk out here," he said, pushing the screen door open. *Good goin', Dad,* Danny thought. *Don't let 'em in the house.*

Ken moved to take one of the chairs, but the officers remained standing, and when Ken saw they weren't going to sit, he didn't either. There was a bit of a staring match until the second cop, the thin, dark-haired one, spoke.

"What were you doing out there on Harbor Island?" he asked.

Oh, shit, Danny thought.

"What? What do you mean?" his father said.

"You and your boy were seen rowing out there," the blond cop said. "We just wondered if you were going there for any special reason."

"It was a nice day. We like to get out on the water."

"Uh-huh." Danny knew that was cop-speak for "We both know you're full of it, but we'll get around to the point eventually." The blond cop made a show of looking at his notebook. "You go there a lot?" he asked.

"Once in a while," Ken told him. "It's nice out there. No cars, no people . . ."

"Uh-huh," the blond cop said again. The radio in the police car, which was parked in the driveway beside the van with its engine running, crackled. The dark-haired cop moved off the porch and went to the vehicle.

"You know anything about the marijuana plants growing out there?" the blond cop asked.

The question took Danny's father by surprise. "What? No." His reaction was so immediate, Danny knew he was telling the truth. Still, this was a worrisome development. There *was* weed in the house, after all, and there were his fireworks to consider.

"Someone reported hearing a disturbance on the island the other night," the blond cop said. "Shots were fired. We went to investigate, and we found a nice little marijuana garden. 'Course some of it had been trampled. But we found mature plants a good six feet high. We pulled 'em up, of course. Lotta dope. You say you don't know anything about it?"

Danny's father rubbed his hands together, a characteristic gesture of nervousness. "Look, Officer, first of all, I don't even own a gun. And second, we just moved here from California. We've only been here since the middle of August. There's no way I could've planted anything out there. I wasn't even around."

"No, but you could've found it."

"I told you, I just go out there for the peace and quiet."

The second officer came back up the steps onto the porch, carrying something in his hand. From his spot by the window, Danny saw that it was a long knife. The cop held it up in front of his father. "You recognize this?" he asked.

The blade was curved and about a foot long. Ken shook his head.

"We found it out on the island," the blond cop said. He let this sink in, watching Ken's face for a reaction. "And there was something else," he added. "We found a deer, right in among the pot plants. A dead deer, slit open from stem to stern." The cop ran a finger down the front of his shirt.

"There's no blood on the knife," Danny's father observed.

"Well, that's what we were wondering about," the dark-haired cop said.

"It looks to me like somebody was guarding those plants, and that deer got a little too close to 'em," the blond cop said. "But the strange thing is, whoever did this just ripped the deer apart and left it there. It were me, I would've dressed her out and hauled her back home, cut her up and put her in the freezer. It's illegal as all get-out to hunt over there, period, in season or out, but I got to think whoever did this is not a hunter. You're not a hunter, are you, Mr. Paxton?"

"No. But I told you, I don't know anything about it—not the deer, not the marijuana plants, not the shots. I'm new in town. I just went to the island because it seemed like it would be something fun to do."

There was a long pause, as no one seemed to know what to say next. The two cops looked at each other, and then at Ken. "You ever see anyone else out there?" the blond one asked finally.

"Nope. Kind of surprising, when you think about it."

"Uh-huh," the cop said, giving away nothing. "How many times you figure you folks been out there, anyway?"

"Oh, two or three," Ken said. "It's a pretty place. And it's not against the law to go out there, is it?"

The cop shook his head. "Long as you don't cut down any trees, or take anything off the island, or build a fire above the high-tide line, the Nature

Conservancy lets people use it. Not many do, though." He looked at the ground, then back up at Danny's father. "You never saw anything suspicious?"

"Nope," Ken said.

The cop turned to his partner. "Well, I guess that's it," he said.

The dark-haired cop, one foot on the top step and the other on the porch itself, nodded once: chin up, chin down.

"Mr. Paxton, if you do see anything out of the ordinary, or if you remember anything you forgot to tell us, you give us a shout, okay?"

"I sure will," Ken said.

The cops left, and a minute later their father came in the door and let out a long sigh of relief.

"What're we going to do now?" Danny asked him.

"We're not going to do anything," he said. "We're going to live our lives."

"But . . . what about the island?"

"What about it? We're not breaking any laws." He chuckled. "It figures someone would be growing pot out there. I wish I *had* found it."

But Ken Paxton's problems got worse before

they got better. On Monday he went to work, where they reprimanded him for missing his assigned Saturday shift. And on Monday evening he went to play rehearsal, from which he returned more depressed than Danny had seen him at any time since they'd left California.

He and Miranda were still up, watching a forgettable action movie starring Bruce Willis, when their father got home. He went to the refrigerator, pulled out a beer, sat down in the tattered red armchair one of his sisters had given him, opened the can, and stared into it. "Shit," he muttered, barely audible. He took a large sip, stared back down into the can. "Shit," he said again.

"Dad, what's wrong?" Miranda asked.

"She's a Yankee fan," he said to the beer can.

"What are you talking about? Who?"

"Michelle. She likes the Yankees. We were talking about the World Series, and she told me she's a Yankee fan." He took another morose sip of beer. He was drinking directly from the can, even though at home he usually used a glass. "First chick I care about in two years, and she has to root for the Yankees."

Danny looked at his sister. He could tell she was trying not to laugh. "Dad, she *is* from New York, right?" Miranda said. "So you can't really blame her."

"Different religions, different musical tastes, different ages—any of those things I could deal with," he said. "It'd be okay if she liked the Mets, or the Orioles, or somebody. Why'd it have to be the Yankees?"

"For God's sake, Dad," Miranda said, "it's only baseball. It's only a game."

"That's where you're wrong," Dad said. "The Yankees are the embodiment of everything that's wrong in the world. Rooting for the Yankees is like rooting for Bill Gates to make another billion dollars. It's like rooting for AMIC to tear down the theater and build another telemarketing center there. It's like . . ." He stopped, aware that Danny and Miranda were rolling their eyes. They had, after all, heard this tirade about a dozen times over the past few baseball seasons.

"Are you saying," Miranda asked, "that her being a Yankee fan is a relationship breaker, while your being a werewolf isn't?"

Their father slumped back in his chair, deflated. "Well, she doesn't know I'm a werewolf," he said.

"And what do you suppose she'll do when she finds out? How do you know she even likes you?"

"She likes me," Dad said.

"She's too young," Miranda said. "And stuck up, besides."

Dad shook his head and stared into the beer can.

"Dad, if you like her, it shouldn't matter who her favorite baseball team is," Miranda said. "I don't think she's right for you, but if you want to ask her out, you should do it and get it over with, instead of agonizing about it."

The Yankees won the World Series in four straight games. Dad went to work at AMIC, and to play rehearsal two evenings a week, and a few days after the end of the Series, baseball ceased to be a regular topic of discussion around the house. He remained interested in Michelle, however, despite their baseball differences, and finally got up the nerve to ask her out on a date. She turned him down.

NINE

Danny wasn't about to spend Halloween doing anything so lame as trick-or-treating, not when there were pumpkins to smash, and not with the arsenal of fireworks at his disposal. His friend Eric was impressed. "Whoa!" he said when Danny showed him his stash. "Where did you get all these?"

"Some of them came from Mexico," Danny told him, "but I got most of this stuff at this giant store we stopped at on the way out here, in Missouri."

"Whoa. You mean you can just walk into a store and buy this stuff?"

"Uh-huh. They've got these big warehouse

stores, all full of fireworks. You can get anything you want there. Cheap, too."

"Man, check *this* out!" Eric held up one of the Power Rockets.

They were hanging in Danny's room, about an hour before dark. Dad hadn't come home from work yet, and Miranda was off with friends. Eric was a little disappointed that she wasn't home, but Danny's collection of fireworks had quickly captured his attention.

"These are pretty cool," Danny said, handing him a small cube with twenty-five projectiles protruding from the top. "You light the fuse at the corner and they all go off, one after the other."

"Man, this is going to be awesome." Eric scooped up a handful of Roman candles, each about a foot long, and held them out in front of him like he'd just discovered Blackbeard's buried treasure. Danny's fireworks collection took up the whole bottom drawer of his dresser, and there were more in the back of his closet. Every single one of them was illegal in Maine, and since Eric had never been out of the state in his life except for one trip to Boston when he was about five, he'd never seen anything like it.

"This is gonna kick ass," he said.

"We can only shoot off a few of them," Danny said. "Could be a long time before I'll be able to get any more. And I gotta save some of them for New Year's."

"We should shoot 'em off up by the water tower," Eric said, rubbing his hands in anticipation. "Someplace where the whole town can see 'em."

"Someplace where we can run away from the cops if they come after us," Danny said.

"Shit, I can outrun any cop in Liverpool," Eric scoffed. Eric was on the cross-country team at school and was good enough to have been invited to the state meet for middle schoolers in Augusta the previous year. He was built for speed—six inches taller than Danny, and skinny, with most of his height in his legs. The kid could run.

"Let's go to the park," Danny suggested. "That way we can run back here if anything happens. My dad's cool about fireworks."

"Your dad's kind of weird, isn't he?"

"What do you mean?"

"Well, everybody I know in this town wants to get the hell out of here. They all talk about going to California. You guys were *there,* and your dad moves you *here.*"

Danny didn't know what to say to that. Eric was a year older, but he hadn't seen much of the world, hadn't experienced many different ways of living. It was a sure thing he'd never walked out of his front door and been panhandled for change by a junkie who spent his nights under a freeway bridge, had never seen police helicopters chase gang members through alleys, had never been stuck in traffic on a four-lane freeway with cars as far as your eyes could see, had never smuggled fireworks over an international border underneath the backseat of a car, had never in fact done or seen dozens of things that had been integral parts of Danny's growing up. Liverpool was Eric's home; it formed the basis of the way he thought about everything and everyone. To Danny it was different. He had seen and lived the differences.

And to his father, it was a refuge. How could

Danny tell his friend that? How could he tell him that his father was a werewolf, that he had come to Liverpool in the hope of being able to live with his curse without killing anyone? Even the kids in California wouldn't have believed *that* story!

"People like different things," he said weakly. "I guess my dad likes Maine."

"Yeah, well, like I said, he's weird," Eric replied. But Danny's answer seemed to satisfy him, and Danny was grateful that he didn't pursue the subject.

His father had the house all decorated for Halloween. They had each carved a jack-o'-lantern to set out on the front porch, though Danny had done a half-assed job on his, because he knew some kid like himself would just come along and smash it. There were witches in the windows and fake spiderwebs above the door, and his dad had laid in a whole bunch of candy, because he had no idea how many trick-or-treaters they would get and he didn't want to run out. Danny loved it that his father got into the spirit of the occasion. He may have been old, but he still had some of the kid he once was inside him.

Of course, he had something else inside him now, Danny reflected, and there wasn't anything childlike about it.

The Moon wasn't full on Halloween, but the Liverpool cops paid their second visit to the house that night.

It must have been the big rocket that got their attention, for the thing was nothing short of spectacular. It took off in a zigzag trajectory, dipped toward the ground, and then rose again, and at the top of its arc it exploded into about a thousand pieces, all of which floated back to Earth like flaming parachutes. Danny was just happy it didn't land in the trees. The rockets were almost impossible to aim. You just dug a shallow hole in the sand, lit the fuse, and then backed off and hoped for the best. They heard somebody shout in the distance, and then they decided to get the hell out of there, because somebody was sure to report it.

Sure enough, a Liverpool police car cruised the park not long after. Danny and Eric crouched behind the bushes until he left, then took a roundabout way back to the house. Danny's father had lots of leftover candy. They were all sitting around munching mini Tootsie Rolls and watching *The Simpsons* on TV when they heard a businesslike knock. Danny's father, thinking it was straggling trick-or-treaters, grabbed the bowl of candy and answered the door.

The cop asked him point-blank if he'd heard any fireworks. Ken looked right back at him in wide-eyed innocence and said, "Didn't hear a thing. We've been besieged by trick-or-treaters."

The cop drew back his head and gave him a strange look, either because he didn't believe him or because he'd never heard anyone use the word *besieged* in everyday conversation. A lot of the people the cops dealt with could barely speak English and said things like "So don't I," and "We was out to my cousin's place."

The cop tilted his head to one side. "Guy next door said he heard several loud explosions," he said. "You didn't hear nothin'?"

"I didn't hear anything," Danny's father said.

The cop looked past him into the living room,

toward Danny and Eric on the couch. "These your kids?" he asked.

"One of 'em is," Ken said, without specifying which one.

"They been here all night?"

"Not yet," Ken said.

The cop didn't laugh. "Just make sure they stay out of trouble. Halloween, a lot of kids think it's fun to go out and raise hell. Seems like it's all in fun, but sometimes people get hurt."

"I'll keep a close eye on 'em, Officer." He held out the bowl. "You want some candy?"

"No, thank you."

November was a dark month, especially in northern latitudes. The trees that had been so colorful a month ago were finally denuded of leaves. From the second-floor window of the house, Danny could now see the bay during the few hours of daylight he was home.

His father was seldom home in the evenings. A typical day at his job began at noon, and he was required to work until eleven at least two nights a week, so Dad and his co-workers could telephone credit card customers all over the country, and eleven o'clock in Maine was only eight o'clock in California. "I can interrupt dinners all night long," Danny's father said.

He got an hour-long break at five, and since AMIC was equipped with a cafeteria and its workers commuted from all over eastern Maine, most of them stayed right there in the building. But Danny's father preferred to come home. He lived only a mile away. Plus he'd discovered that the Sci-Fi Channel showed the original *Star Trek* every weeknight from five to six. Ken could come home, turn on the TV a couple of minutes into the show, whip up something to eat, and watch all but the very end before heading back to work. This got him in trouble a couple of times. One evening he insisted on staying for the end of the episode in which Kirk defeated the *Nomad* space probe with what Spock termed "a dazzling display of logic" (Danny was dismayed to discover that his dad knew the line), and drew a formal reprimand from his supervisor.

Other evenings he went to the theater to

rehearse. He was still mooning over Michelle, but now he had the Moon to worry about. It would be full four days before opening night, and he had gotten into the bad graces of the director by telling him he would have to miss the dress rehearsal.

"I don't know what the big deal is," he said one evening as he scarfed down a bowl of macaroni and cheese while watching Captain Kirk battle a lizard-like monster on a planet littered with sulphur deposits and diamonds. "I'm only in one scene. It's not like I have to carry the show or anything. The audience is gonna be watching Michelle."

"Dad, forget about her," said Miranda.

Captain Kirk, his shirt ripped and his face smeared with dirt, was scooping some powder into a hollow tube as the lizard creature came over a rise. The station cut to a commercial. Dad took his empty bowl into the kitchen and put on his coat. "Gotta get back to work," he said. "Tell me how it ends."

"Kirk dies," Danny piped up. "Isn't this the last episode they ever made?"

His father laughed. He could probably recite the ending from memory, but it still pained him that his responsibility as the family breadwinner precluded him from sticking around and watching it for the seventy-ninth time. "See you guys around midnight," he said, and walked out into the dark November night.

The Moon wasn't going to wait. Play or no play, job or no job, girl or no girl, cops or no cops—when the Moon got full again, Danny's father would have to safeguard the town of Liverpool from the beast he would become. And that meant going out to the island.

What was the alternative? Chain him to the sewer pipe in the basement? Drive him into the north Maine woods and let him chase moose? Although they had been living with their father's affliction for several months now, Danny and Miranda had never actually *seen* him in the werewolf state. They had no idea what he could do. Perhaps he could rip that sewer pipe from the foundation, and wouldn't *that* be a mess?

But if this month's trip to the island was seen and aroused suspicion, what would prevent some curious redneck from following them out there to see what was going on? He'd have a gun, of course, and if confronted would undoubtedly, as the saying went, shoot first and ask questions later.

All this went through Danny's mind as the full moon approached, and he knew that Miranda was worried too. They talked about it, in the evenings when their dad wasn't home, in a circle of unre-solved conversations between homework and TV. They considered calling their mother for advice—neither one had used any of the stationery she'd given them—but Mom had never been much in the reliability department. The teen years were sup-posed to be a time of stress and changes; you were supposed to be filled with anxiety and angst and not know what to do in a whole smorgasbord of situations. But you were also supposed to be secure in the knowledge that your parents were watching out for you, that if you really messed up, they would be able to call on resources you could only imagine, and they would make things, if not all right, at least survivable. You weren't supposed to have your parents rely on *you*. Yet that's exactly how Danny felt—that if he didn't protect his father, he would be responsible for some horrible tragedy.

His dad didn't know how he was going to handle it at work either. Because of the play and his frequent *Star Trek*–induced lateness in getting back from his dinner break, he hesitated to ask for three consecutive evenings off so that he could transform into a werewolf. AMIC was strict about schedules for new hires. Once you'd been there awhile, Danny's father explained, you could get sick or have a parent die or your car could break down, but in the first few months on the job those things weren't easily tolerated. It was a test of loyalty, Dad said. The company wanted to make sure you were willing to put credit card telephone transactions ahead of everything else. Once you'd proven yourself, once it had become second nature to put on a tie and the little gold AMIC lapel pin and proudly display your AMIC parking decal in the center of your windshield and leave your badge with your mug shot on it dangling from your coat when you stopped at the store for groceries—once they *had* you, in other words—

they were willing to let you off the leash a little. But not in the first couple of months.

So he didn't tell his boss in advance that he needed those evenings off. He didn't plan ahead for them at all. And that was totally true to his nature. He approached the new reality of his life as a werewolf in the same seat-of-the-pants fashion, hoping for the best, taking precautions to prevent himself from killing anyone, but without any fallback strategy in case something went wrong.

It was just Dad's dumb luck that the weather cooperated and a big rainstorm blew in on the first night of the full moon. The few remaining leaves were swept from the trees and blasted into the ditches along the side of the road. The bay was frothed with whitecaps; you couldn't even see across to Harbor Island, let alone take a boat out there. Ken decided to go to work, after watching the Weather Channel and ascertaining that the storm was likely to last a day or two. It got dark at four thirty because of the thick cloud cover. The Moon might as well have been orbiting Venus for all they would see of it that night. Their father came home, watched a really stupid *Star Trek* episode in which Abe Lincoln appeared on a chair in space, and went back out into the squall. He came home at midnight and slept without incident. In the morning it was still raining.

All during school that day, Danny kept looking out the window, praying that the storm would continue. But unfortunately the rain began letting up halfway though algebra and stopped completely during world history. Danny's mind was a long way from the Norman invasion of 1066 as he gazed out the window at the clearing sky and realized that he had his own personal English Channel to cross.

Sure enough, when the bus let him off, Dad was home, sitting at the kitchen table with a beer and poring over an almanac he'd bought at the bookstore on Main Street the week they moved to Liverpool. "I called in sick," he said. "You're going to have to take me out to the island."

"What if someone sees us?" Danny said.

"That's the good news," his father replied. He jabbed a finger into the almanac. "The Moon was actually full yesterday at one in the afternoon. And since it's the second night, it won't rise until nearly an hour after sunset. We can wait until dusk." He looked up and beamed. "And because of the way the Moon's orbit is tilted in respect to the ecliptic this month, tomorrow night I shouldn't be affected at all!"

"Great," Danny managed to say.

"How do you know all this?" Miranda asked him skeptically.

"I've been on the phone with Sid," Dad said. "He's been studying this stuff for years."

"You mean the old guy at Pismo Beach?" Danny asked.

His father nodded. "He's kept charts over the years, and he says he's never seen the werewolf appear more than forty-eight hours before or after the time of true full moon, when the Moon is at the point in its orbit exactly opposite the Sun. So if we can get through tonight, we should be safe for another month."

"You mean," Miranda said, "the *town* should be safe."

"Well, yeah," Dad said.

○ ☾ ◑ ☽ ☽ ○ ◐ ● ◗

The wind had died down but the sea was still choppy when they rowed him out to the island. The sky glowed red over the land behind them, and the first stars had appeared, but it was almost dark and there was no Moon. If anyone had been looking out a window they would have had a hard time spotting the rowboat in the gathering darkness. Danny put his back into his rowing as the dinghy bounced over the ragged waves. Occasionally one of the oars caught the tip of a wave as he drew it back, splashing Miranda in the bow. "Splash me again," she finally said, "and I'm gonna come into your room when you're fast asleep tonight and dump a glass of water on your head." But Danny was glad to have her along. The added weight and its even distribution in the boat made rowing easier, and although he didn't admit it to her or to their father, he would have been a little scared to row back to shore alone in the dark.

Ken sat in the stern, looking nervously ahead. His small knapsack, containing a candy bar, a plastic bottle of orange juice, and a change of clothes for the morning, lay at his feet. Even though the oncoming night was chilly, Danny could see sweat on his forehead. Behind the trees on the island the sky glowed, and the glow grew brighter each time he glanced over his shoulder to make sure the island was still there. Dad had taught him the trick of keeping the stern aligned with a point on the opposite shore, so he really didn't need to keep turning around and looking, but he craved the reassurance of his destination. From the glow in the sky and his father's increasing nervousness, he knew they didn't have much time.

After what seemed like hours, but could only have been a little more than thirty minutes, the boat crunched against the rocky bottom of the landing place on the island. Dad jumped out into six inches of water and grabbed his pack from the bottom of the boat. Miranda hopped out too, with the painter, onto dry land. The tide was halfway up and rising. The Moon was also rising. In seconds the glow behind the trees would be replaced by the Moon itself. Already the stars had disappeared from the eastern half of the sky.

Ken waded ashore and turned toward Danny

to speak. Something invisible smacked him between the eyes. He staggered, then threw the knapsack as hard as he could up onto the bank. He looked at his children, his eyes wild. His hands flew to his head, and he sank to his knees. "Go!" he cried, his voice full of gravel.

"Dad—"

"Get out of here!" he roared. "Go, while you still can!"

Danny heard something rip, and a second later realized that it was the shoulder of his father's denim jacket as he tore it off. He rose to one knee and roared again, but this time there were no comprehensible words. His face contorted in agony. Miranda's eyes were huge. "Morning!" their father rasped. "Here . . . now *go!* Aaaaaaah!"

And that was when Danny actually *saw* his face change, and knew, down in his bones *knew* that everything the old man on Pismo Beach had told them was true. For his father's face did not simply change expression; no, it changed *shape,* it changed its very physical structure, right before Danny's eyes, until it was the face of his father no longer.

Miranda was already moving, throwing the painter back into the boat, pushing the bow back into the water. "Get in, Danny, *get in!*" Their father was now rolling around on the ground, making incoherent animal noises. "Come on!" Danny's sister cried. He grabbed the discarded jacket—God knew why—and threw it into the boat. Miranda ran to the stern. Danny gave the bow a mighty push and the dinghy floated free. He grabbed the oars, backed with one arm and pulled with the other, and the boat turned. Pulled away from the shore. The figure on the shore rose to its feet and took a couple of steps toward the water.

"Go!" Miranda screamed.

Danny splashed her with his first panicked stroke, but she didn't seem to care. He pulled the oars through the water twice, three times, more, as hard and as fast as he could. He saw the beast on the shore—which only moments ago had been recognizable as his father—wade out to waist level and stop as Danny increased the distance between them. For a panicked moment he thought their

151

shapeshifted father meant to swim after them. But then he turned his face to the rising Moon and howled. The harrowing sound pierced the night, and Danny saw his sister shiver. Then he saw the creature turn back toward the shore. He saw him walk out of the water, drop to his knees, and shake like a dog. He saw water fly from fur. He saw the thing rise up on two legs again and look out at the little boat. He heard the beast bay at the Moon once more, and then he saw it drop to all fours and bound up into the trees.

The bay was now bathed in yellow moonlight. Danny hunched forward over the oars and indulged in several deep breaths before he resumed rowing, this time steadily, methodically, and without panic, toward the mainland. Perhaps someone in the houses on the shore had heard their father's howls, and had one or more of them looked out one of their picture windows, they might have seen a small boat with two badly scared young people in it, silhouetted against the rising Moon. They were halfway across before either of them spoke.

"He really *is* a werewolf," Miranda said.

"Yes," Danny said. He stopped rowing for a minute and looked over his shoulder at the lights of the town. "Those people have no idea. They don't know how lucky they are."

TEN

In mid-November the AMIC corporation announced it would purchase sixty acres of land along Route 1 in Liverpool for the purpose of constructing a second customer service center, which would bring nearly a thousand new jobs to Midcoast Maine. The purchase was widely regarded as a Good Thing.

Within a week the old farm buildings were gone, and plans appeared in the local paper showing the layout of the new AMIC complex. It was obvious that those plans had existed for some time, and that AMIC had released the news of its expansion to the media only after it was a done deal and no serious opposition could be raised.

What small anti-AMIC sentiment there was confined itself to word-of-mouth and the occasional letter to the editor in the local paper. The new construction was a boon to landlords, who were already jacking up rents to take advantage of the higher wages AMIC could afford to pay, thereby squeezing out residents who had to subsist on the traditional low-paying service and production jobs that had always been the backbone of the area's rural economy. There was plenty of work—the fish-packing factory had been forced to raise its starting wage to seven dollars per hour to get people to fill the chronic shortage of hands on the packing line—and that seemed like a good thing on paper. Unemployment was at an all-time low. But you could work forty hours a week and still not have enough money for rent and groceries—unless you worked for AMIC.

There were odd incidents that the local people laughed about. Across the highway from the new center, Raymond Astbury sold snowmobiles, four-wheelers, and motorcycles, as well as assorted other junk he had collected over the years. It was one of those ramshackle Maine businesses, run out of an old farmhouse with constantly changing inventory. Most visible from the road was the collection of old bicycles that dominated the front lawn from spring thaw to first snow. If you needed a cheap bike on which to get around Liverpool, Raymond's was the place to go. It wasn't a yard sale, exactly, but it looked like one. Not a unique characteristic of businesses along coastal Route 1, but apparently not in keeping with the clean, corporate image AMIC wanted to project to its employees and contractors and anyone else who happened to drive by its spanking new facility. One day a man in a suit approached Astbury and offered to buy the entire collection of bicycles— some three or four dozen. He offered a decent price, and Astbury accepted the offer. The man in the suit was from AMIC, of course, and the bikes were loaded into the bed of a blue-and-silver truck and carted away to the city dump. Unbeknownst to AMIC, however, the chief attendant at the dump was Raymond Astbury's cousin. He promptly called Raymond and asked if he would like his bikes back. The bikes returned, after an absence of only a day, and Raymond Astbury made several hundred dollars.

Ken's play opened the weekend before Thanksgiving. He was a little nervous, he admitted to Danny, even though he had only three lines, because he'd missed the dress rehearsal. A lot of things had gone wrong, and the director was angry at everybody. Ken's bosses at AMIC weren't pleased either. He had already missed time for rehearsals, and he had called in sick twice during his first two months. On the day of the play he received a written warning that further unexcused absences could negatively affect his future with the company.

Thanksgiving—which fell in the middle of the play's two weekends of performances—was a big family reunion at the grandparents' house. The place was filled with cousins and stepparents and uncles and aunts, none of whom Danny and Miranda knew well. Their father had three sisters, all of whom had been divorced and remarried at least once. It was very confusing trying to figure out who was related to whom through what sibling relationship. Everybody called one another by their first names.

But there was a Ping-Pong table in the basement, and the house was near the shore, and the weather was clear. Cold, but clear. Danny and his cousin Bryan wrote their names on the beach with rocks and driftwood for the benefit of any passing helicopters; when they got cold they went inside and played Ping-Pong and computer games. Danny's grandmother cooked a gargantuan turkey and a plethora of side dishes, with pumpkin pie for dessert. They all stuffed themselves. Danny's father said, "If you aren't in pain when you leave the table, you haven't properly celebrated Thanksgiving." Everyone judged the holiday properly celebrated.

Danny's father had to endure a few questions about his employment at AMIC, and Gram wanted to know how the kids were doing at their new school in their new state and town. Dad deflected the talk about AMIC by telling them about the play, which had drawn less than full houses during its first weekend. "I'm only in one scene," he said, "but it's the first acting I've done since high school. Besides, it's a pretty good play. You should come—all of you."

It was nearly midnight when they left. They had to get back because Dad had to work the day after Thanksgiving—a good day to bug people on the phone, as many would be home trying to enjoy a four-day holiday weekend. He hadn't told his family that he was now on probation.

Kat, one of his sisters, was staying over with her brood; she told Ken that she would swing by on the way back to Vermont and maybe see the play. They descended on the house in Liverpool the following afternoon, but when Kat's husband saw the disclaimer on the poster Ken produced ("Due to strong language and sexual content, this show is not appropriate for children"), he convinced her to continue their trip before it got dark. Kat shrugged, hugged Danny's father, and said, "Maybe next time."

Danny was glad that his father had never tried to protect him from things the adult world deemed "inappropriate." The sexual content consisted of a couple of suggestive scenes with fully clothed

159

actors, and two kisses. You saw more skin on MTV. Kat's youngest kid was ten, and what ten-year-old hadn't heard all the dirty words on a school playground? The only thing the warning on the poster did, Danny thought, was keep people away.

None of the family came to see the play. It closed that Sunday after drawing thin audiences for most of the shows. Danny went down to help with the strike of the set and got to collect some boards he intended to make into a bookshelf in his room. Afterward his father went to a cast party, from which he returned home early. The next day it was as though the play had never happened. School, an empty house, his dad home for *Star Trek* and out again. Danny wished it would snow. Miranda, surprisingly, grew morose over this. "If we're going to live in Maine," she said, "we ought to at least have a white Christmas." Instead the land remained hard, lumpy, and brown.

Most of the boats were now gone from the harbor. The town hauled in its barnacle-encrusted floats and stacked them in the parking lots the tourists used in the summer. This gave the harbor

160

a barren look, as the docks ended at empty space, and bare poles stuck up out of the water where the floats had been. Danny's father kept the dinghy down at the park and made sure to go rowing every few days in spite of the cold. They would still have to go out to the island, he said, and their trips would be less noteworthy if it appeared that he rowed regularly, for exercise. "Like some people run all the time, no matter how cold it is," he explained. Indeed, Danny saw people running in the mornings, bundled up in about five sweatshirts and wool hats and thick mittens, each breath a white cloud. Danny thought they were nuts. He could only imagine what the townspeople must think of his father.

He rowed in the mornings, in boots and thick mittens, with a wool scarf wrapped around his face. Danny and Miranda didn't see him spend much time at the computer any more. The dream of becoming a screenwriter seemed to be fading faster than the autumn daylight. They didn't see much of their father at all, in fact, except on weekends and in the mornings before school, because his job kept him out of the house until late into the cold, starry nights.

"I hate my job," he said into his coffee cup one morning.

"Would you rather be packing fish?" Miranda shot back.

"No, but at least it's honest work. You can eat fish."

"You're making good money, Dad."

"I'm still going to have to get another job, during regular business hours. This staying out till eleven at night so I can call credit card customers on the West Coast is for the birds."

"A day job would be good," Danny said, trying to be helpful. "The full moon's only up at night."

"The next full moon," their father said, "is on the winter solstice. The longest night of the year."

The coast of Maine is about halfway between the equator and the North Pole. San Diego, where Danny had spent every winter of his life before this one, lies near the thirty-third parallel, where the seasonal difference in daylight is not nearly as noticeable.

The Earth's axis of rotation is tilted twenty-four degrees from the plane of its orbit around the Sun, and as every schoolchild knows, this is the reason for the seasons. The winter solstice, December 21, occurs at the point in the Earth's orbit when the North Pole points directly away from the Sun. Miranda maintained that thousands of years before anybody heard of Jesus, our animal-skin-clad ancestors were so happy to see the shortening of the days reversed that they built bonfires and had wild, drunken parties to celebrate, and that the Christians just folded this tradition into their own. That's why there wasn't any room at the inn, she said—because everyone was in town for the big solstice party.

But this year's winter solstice was noteworthy, because it coincided so closely with the full moon, and it was supposed to be the biggest, brightest, baddest full moon of the century, as well as the last. (Danny's father had spent most of 1999 pointing out to everyone that the twentieth century would not end until December 31, 2000, despite the premature millennial celebrations.) The

Moon was unusually close to the Earth in its orbit, and the Earth, believe it or not, is always closest to the Sun in late December and early January. So not only would the Moon appear huge in the sky, it would be in the sky for something like sixteen hours, the length of the longest night of the year.

And then the cold intensified, until even the native Mainers remarked upon it. The temperature plummeted to well below freezing and stayed there, even in the middle of the day. The sky was a shade of deep blue that Danny had never seen before. Ice crystals coated the windows, and everyone wore sweaters and heavy socks around the house. The furnace blasted away in the basement; Danny's father fretted about pipes freezing. It was fortunate that he didn't have to get up first thing in the morning and go to his job, for the car started only with the greatest reluctance, and sometimes not until the third or fourth attempt. "It's just an early cold snap," their father kept telling them. "It'll break." But it didn't.

By mid-December everyone was talking about the continuing cold. The ground crunched underfoot. The ponds froze, and kids brought out skates and hockey sticks. Dad, with extra money to spend for once in his life, bought three pairs of skates and astonished Danny and Miranda by doing backward figure eights and tight turns while they stumbled around, feeling like idiots and trying not to fall. Until then they'd had no idea that their father could ice-skate. "Don't forget, I grew up in a cold climate," he said, laughing gently at their bewildered faces.

Danny watched other kids playing hockey and was occasionally invited to participate. He had always thought hockey was a dumb sport, because the few games he had seen on TV had been highlighted by fights in which the players pulled one another's jerseys over their heads and slugged away blindly. But on the frozen surface of the Swamp he gained a new appreciation for the game. You had to think about staying upright on skates and making them go where you wanted them to, and *then* you had to think about passing and shooting the puck. It was harder than it looked.

Skating distracted his father from the looming

threat of the approaching full moon, but Danny could tell that he was anxious. The Moon grew larger each night, and the cold showed no signs of abating. They made an attempt to get into the spirit of the Christmas season. They cut and decorated a tree and hung a wreath on the door, and they put greens around the house. But to Danny it felt like these rituals were done, not with a sense of joy, but of obligation. They did them out of a desperate need for normalcy, because they wanted to be like everybody else. But their holiday could not possibly be like everybody else's. Their mother was in California, and their father was a werewolf.

Five days before the solstice, they took a shopping trip to the Maine Mall in Portland. It was jammed with holiday shoppers. They bought gifts for their mother and all the members of their extended family, but Ken spent most of his time and money at the camping supply store, where he bought a heavy bivouac bag, a kerosene heater, three complete sets of long underwear, a cookstove and camping pans, a pile of high-energy fruit bars and freeze-dried food, and enough cold-weather survival gear to equip an expedition up Mount Everest. He dropped hundreds of dollars in that one store.

On the drive back up Route 1 he explained his thinking to Danny and Miranda. "We'll take this stuff out to the island while it's still dark," he said. "Because if anyone sees us, they'll think we're nuts, and they'll talk. You're gonna have to leave me out there for a couple of days."

"Dad! You'll freeze to death!" Miranda cried.

He shook his head. "I can keep that cave pretty warm," he said, "and that bag I bought is good down to forty below. I won't be able to have a fire, because people on shore would see the smoke. And I can't have anyone seeing you row out there either. I've got to stay out there until the Moon is past full. Until the town is safe."

"How will we know that *you're* safe?" Danny asked him.

"You'll just have to trust me," he said. "You can pick me up before dawn on the day before Christmas. After midnight the Moon should be far enough past full that I'll be human again." He smiled, but the worry didn't leave his eyes. "And then we'll really have something to celebrate."

"And what about January, and February, and March?" Danny asked. "It's going to be winter for a long time."

"One month at a time, son. That's all I can do—take it one month at a time."

They watched the Weather Channel around the clock for the next couple of days. Icy blue animated arrows swirled down from the Canadian heartland and smothered New England as a succession of well-dressed weathermen and weatherwomen predicted clear skies and record low temperatures throughout the weekend of the solstice. Danny flashed back to that picture of the frozen bay in the AMIC lobby and remembered the words of the security guard: "It hasn't happened in fifty years." Nonetheless he felt a vast sense of relief each morning when he went to the upstairs window and saw for himself that the water between the shore and Harbor Island was still open.

There was ice all along the shore when Danny

168

took his father out to the island in the predawn darkness of December 21. Ocean ice is strange. It has a spongy quality at first, as though it freezes reluctantly, and only hardens over time as the temperature drops well below freezing. Because the tide goes in and out, huge tilted graduation caps are left perched on top of rocks, and sheets of ice attached to the shore sag as the water flows out from beneath them. It was half-tide when they set out from the shore in darkness; the ice covering extended from the high-water mark out a good stone's throw into the bay. Danny skipped a rock and watched it skitter along the solid surface before dropping off into the black water beyond.

He had never felt such cold. He was wearing thermal underwear, a turtleneck, a sweater, a heavy winter jacket, and thick wool mittens and hat. The only skin exposed to the ravaging temperature was his face, in which he lost feeling almost immediately. His toes, despite thick socks and heavy boots, throbbed in protest. Grimly, wordlessly, they loaded all his father's equipment into the dinghy and slid it down over the ice toward the water. Ken volunteered to row out. The weight of the boat easily broke through the thin sheet of ice at the water's edge; the oars poked holes in it until they were out into clear water.

There wasn't a breath of wind. Even the smallest breeze would have made the trip unbearable. Danny sat in the stern and watched his father row, rocking back and forth in time to his rhythm, not wanting to keep completely still lest he freeze in that position. It was too cold to talk. Danny could see the faint glow of approaching dawn in the sky beyond the island, and although this was the shortest day of the year, he knew it would be the longest day of his father's life.

The dinghy crunched into ice several boat lengths from the shore of the island. Ken had to stand up and poke the oars through the ice and pole the boat to shore. "Dad, this is nuts," Danny said, and felt gratified that his vocal cords hadn't frozen.

"It beats the alternative," his father replied. The boat settled against the ice onshore. He jumped out with the painter and almost went flying before his boots gained a purchase on the slippery surface. Danny helped him carry his stuff up past the high-tide line. It was weird to see ice covering the shore and bare ground beyond, for it still had not snowed. Danny would have preferred a blizzard to this biting cold.

When everything was unloaded, Danny and his father stood a small distance apart and looked at each other, their breath rising in twin clouds of steam. "I'll be all right," Ken said, sensing that Danny doubted it, perhaps doubting it himself. "I'll see you in three days."

Three days, Danny thought, out alone on this patch of tree-covered rock, with a heater and a supply of kerosene to keep him warm during the few hours when the Sun was above the horizon. And the beast within him would run his body through the interminable nights when the Moon ruled. *Could a werewolf freeze to death?*

The question hung unspoken between them. "Go on," his father said finally. "It's gonna be light soon." They hugged like two Eskimos through their many layers of padding.

"Good luck, Dad," Danny mumbled into the folds of his father's parka.

"Take good care of your sister." His father patted the side of his head with a bulky mitten, and then they walked down to the dinghy. His father pushed the boat off; Danny chopped at the ice with his oars until he was in clear water. As he pulled away from the shore, his father turned back toward the pile of survival gear and began to sort through it.

Danny rowed briskly and steadily to keep back the cold. His father soon disappeared into the trees on the island, carrying the heater and a can of kerosene. The sky was losing the darkness, though a few lingering bright stars were still visible. Looking over his shoulder, Danny could see the approaching dawn reflected in the windows of the hulking main building of the AMIC corporation. A skin of ice had formed on the water in front of it, and the sky reflected off that, too.

Danny got to shore and pulled the boat up over the ice and secured it in its normal spot. He looked back out at Harbor Island. Dawn was rapidly coming on, but there was something else—a fuzzing of outlines that struck him as eerily strange in the gripping cold. His numbed face and fingers and toes urged him to get back to the house and heat as quickly as possible, but he stood on the shore for several minutes as the sky above turned from indigo to cobalt and a dry mist rose from the sea. Fascinated, he watched as the mist obscured the far shore of the bay and then swallowed Harbor Island. Then he realized what it was. Sea smoke, his father had called it. You see it on frigid mornings when the surface of the water is warmer than the air. Danny was very glad he had gotten to shore before it had enveloped the dinghy, because he might have been lost out there without points of reference, and rowed around in circles until he collapsed from exhaustion and succumbed to fear or frostbite or both. He clenched and unclenched his fists inside his mittens, trying to coax some blood into his frozen fingertips, and then he hurried off toward the house, not running, but walking as fast as he could.

It was Friday. That night Miranda went to the

movies with several of her friends, but Danny stayed home. He pulled a chair up to the upstairs window and watched through the outline of ice crystals as the Moon came up over the bay. It was huge—as huge as the secret his family harbored, out on the island, in the body and soul of his father.

There was still no wind. Danny put on his big winter jacket and opened the door to the porch. The air stabbed at the insides of his lungs with icy shards of oxygen as he inhaled it in tiny sips. He could see the lights of the Chevron station down the street and the stars of the Big Dipper above, but the sky was dominated by the Moon. A couple of cars went by, and Danny heard a door open and close—punctuation to the silence.

But there was another sound, something faint yet distinct, from the direction of the water. A deep, mysterious sound, almost a groan, like the skin of an animal stretched tightly over a drum and then loosened as fingers played across it. Then a snap, like someone cracking a whip, followed by more otherworldly groaning sounds. The hair on the back of Danny's neck prickled, and he shivered in the cold. And then he realized what it was—the water in the bay freezing. *It hasn't happened in fifty years,* the security guard had said. But everyone in town was talking about the cold.

And then, far off in the distance, he heard something else, drifting over the frigid water and the frozen landscape, carrying through the stilled air. Any animal with any sense must have been hunkered down in its den, or nest, or burrow, curled against its mate or siblings, hoarding warmth. But somewhere out there, in a voice haunting and musical, something was baying at the Moon.

Dad.

ELEVEN

Danny was asleep on the couch, underneath his thermal sleeping bag, when Miranda came home. He had been watching TV and dozed off. He jumped at the sound of the door and shivered in the blast of cold air it admitted.

"Man, is it cold out there!" his sister exclaimed. "I didn't know we were moving to the *North Pole,* for Christ's sake!"

Her face was bright pink. But there was something else, something in her eyes—they were as pink as her cheeks. Because Danny had been asleep, it took him a few seconds to figure it out.

"You're stoned, aren't you?" he said, gathering

the sleeping bag up around his chest. "You've been into Dad's stash!"

Miranda pulled off her white knitted hat and threw it into a chair. She shook her hair loose and unwrapped the wool scarf from around her neck. "Do you think I need *Dad* to find weed in this town?" she snorted, as she started to unzip her coat. "Everybody and his brother grows it. Half your classmates are stoners."

"Dad wouldn't like it if he knew you were smoking," Danny said.

"So what? It's his fault anyway, for bringing us to this Arctic wilderness. There's nothing to *do* here but get high. Reality *sucks*. Is there anything to eat?"

She tossed her coat into the same chair as her hat, and stalked off into the kitchen. Danny heard the refrigerator door open. "Besides," she called, "I don't see *him* setting such a great example. He's not even here. I could have stayed out all night if I'd wanted to. I could've been out gangbanging the *football team,* and there's not a damn thing he could do about it."

"You know why he isn't here, Miranda," Danny said softly.

"Right." She banged around some more, opening drawers and cupboards. Danny heard her strike a match to light the stove. Her face appeared around the corner. "You know," she said, "just because he's a werewolf shouldn't mean that *we* have to suffer. He should've left us with Mom. Think about it. She goes off on her three-day binges and abandons us. But how long is Dad gonna be out on the island? Three days. And we're left alone. I don't see the difference."

Danny couldn't think of anything to say in reply to this, so he turned his attention to the TV. An elephant stomped through the African savannah, yanking off tree branches as it went and stuffing them into its mouth. Danny had been watching a documentary on the hunting habits of lions on the Discovery Channel before falling asleep, perhaps thinking that pictures of Africa would make him feel slightly warmer.

"Where the hell are the brownies?" his sister called from the kitchen.

"We finished 'em yesterday, remember?"

"Damn it!" More pots and pans rattled; Miranda was foraging through the kitchen every bit as recklessly as the elephant on TV.

"What time is it, anyway?" Danny asked.

"I don't know, midnight?"

"Look at the clock on the stove," Danny suggested.

A pause. "It's 12:07," his sister said.

Pretty soon she came back into the living room with a jam-covered English muffin and a cup of hot chocolate, and made Danny make room for her on the couch. She sat down beside him and changed the channel.

"Hey!" he protested. "I was watching that!"

"No, you weren't. You were asleep. Besides, if you've seen one elephant, you've seen them all." She turned to MTV, which was playing a video by some big-haired rock band. The song throbbed over a series of quick cuts between a concert performance and a street scene in which the members of the band were being chased through a city by a mob of teenage girls. When the song ended, Miranda

insisted on sitting through ten minutes of commer-
cials filmed in much the same style as the video.

"Forget this," Danny said. "I'm going to bed."
He got up off the couch.

"Yeah, this is schlock," Miranda said, and hit
the OFF button on the remote.

As the TV went silent, there was that strange,
elongated drumbeat sound in the distance, followed by a loud crack. They both heard it and
looked at each other.

"What was *that*?" Miranda said.

"I think it's the water in the bay freezing,"
Danny told her. "I've been hearing it all night. You
know, ice expands. Like that time Dad put a beer
in the freezer and forgot about it. . . ."

"I remember. It broke the bottle."

"When a pond freezes over, sometimes you see
big cracks in it," Danny said. "Because the ice
expands, and it's got no place to go. It gets
squeezed between the sides. Like the bay between
here and Harbor Island."

Miranda's face went pale. "You think the bay's
going to freeze over?"

"Well, it's pretty damn cold."

"Yeah, but . . . Dad's out there!"

"The guy at AMIC said it hadn't happened for fifty years, remember?"

"It probably hasn't been this cold in fifty years! Danny, what if the bay *does* freeze over? I mean, solid enough to walk on?"

Danny felt the house grow colder around him and his sister. "It'll never happen," he said, trying to reassure himself as much as Miranda. "The tide goes in and out of there. That water's constantly moving. And salt water freezes at a lower temperature anyway."

"But it does freeze. It's done it before. It was frozen around the edges this morning. Suppose it freezes all the way across? Suppose Dad gets it into his werewolf head to come over and check out the town?"

"He won't do that," Danny said. "You saw all the precautions he took. The heater, the big mummy bag . . ."

"But when he changes, all that rational thought goes out the window! Remember the cattle mutilations in Kansas? The Mexicans in California?" Miranda bit her lower lip. Danny wondered if she was going to cry. Tentatively he put his arms around her. Under normal circumstances she would have pushed him away. But these were not normal circumstances.

"I'm scared," she whispered.

"Me too."

"Wanna sleep in the living room? There's probably a late movie on or something."

"Okay."

They spread out the couch cushions on the floor and laid their pillows and sleeping bags on top of them, turned up the thermostat, and browsed the channels until they came up with a movie that was acceptable to both of them. Danny wouldn't remember much of it, because within half an hour he was asleep, comforted by the presence of his sister beside him. When he woke again it was daylight.

He got up, turned off the TV, dressed, and decided to let his sister sleep. Frost covered most of the windows; the crystals glinted in the early-morning sunlight. Danny bundled up and walked down to the park. Ice covered the entire shoreline. It was low tide. The bay hadn't frozen all the way over, not yet—there was a thin channel of open water between the sheet of ice extending out from the shore and a similar sheet that surrounded Harbor Island. The ice came all the way up to the high-tide line, broken here and there by rocks and large cracks. Danny slid along the solid surface until it leveled out, and he knew he was over water. Gingerly he continued outward from the shore. It felt solid. He walked out a little farther. There was still no give beneath his feet. He jumped up and down, once—nothing happened. He didn't want to walk too far out, because there might be weak spots, for all he knew. He had heard stories of people falling through the ice and freezing to death, but it looked solid for quite a distance from shore.

And it sure as hell wasn't getting any warmer. The weak December Sun sat low in the southern sky, over the outer bay, on its lowest arc across the sky all year. Tomorrow it would rise imperceptibly farther north, and set a minute or two later, and the next day it would crawl slightly northward again, and again and again as the Earth swung back around toward the vernal equinox. But that was no help to Danny's father, out on the island. He would be back in human form by now, in the wan daylight, huddled in his cave by the kerosene heater, trying to keep the cold from killing him. How Danny wished he could go out there, to make sure he was all right!

"Oh, what a mess we're in," he whispered through the scarf he had wrapped around his face. He couldn't possibly get to the island to rescue his father, not with the bay half frozen. He would have to drag the dinghy out onto the ice, get in, and somehow guide it to open water. Then he would need to negotiate the ice on the other side. It would have to warm up before Christmas, that was all.

But there were still two nights of the full moon to get through. Two long nights.

Miranda was in the kitchen making pancakes when Danny got back to the house. The smell made the house seem warmer. "I'm going to Crystal's tonight," his sister told him as she served him a plate. "She's renting some movies and having a bunch of girls over, and we're gonna crash out in her den. There's fish sticks and fries you can heat up for dinner. Don't burn the house down."

"You're gonna leave me here by myself?"

"Sure. You can handle it."

"But Dad said—"

"Dad said for us to look after each other. Okay, I'm telling you I'll be at Crystal's. You're not scared of being alone in the house for one night, are you? What's gonna happen?"

Danny looked at the floor. He *was* scared. Miranda could be a pain, but he'd discovered he liked having her around.

"Look, I'm worried about Dad too," she said softly. "But there's nothing we can do about it until the full moon passes. He'll either be okay or he won't. But it'll drive me crazy to just sit around this house and think about it every minute. Maybe you could go over to Eric's or something."

Danny shook his head. "I doubt it," he said. "He got in trouble last week for fighting at school. His mother hasn't been letting him have overnight guests."

"Nice friends you got there," Miranda said.

"It wasn't his fault. Some kid was picking on his little brother. You can't hold it against him that he sticks up for his brother."

Miranda smiled. "No, I guess not," she said. "I'll leave Crystal's phone number. You can call me if anything comes up. But nothing is going to come up. Okay?"

"Okay," Danny said. But he wasn't happy about it.

When she left, just after noon, the silence of the empty house closed in around him. He turned on the TV, but there was nothing on but cartoons and cooking shows. He decided to call Eric. "I'm bored," he said. "What're you doing?"

"There's a hockey game up at the Swamp," Eric replied. "Wanna come?"

"You know I can't skate," Danny said. "I'm from California."

"Who cares? There's gonna be a bonfire after. I'll come by your house on the way. Bring your skates; we might need extra players."

"Eric, I don't even own a hockey stick."

"I got an extra one you can use. See you in about half an hour." Before Danny could protest any further, he hung up.

Well, it was better than hanging around the house by himself, worrying about his father. There was a large lean-to on the shore of the Swamp, with a bench where kids could sit and put on their skates. Several kids were already there when Danny and Eric arrived. Some were lacing up their skates; others gathered dead branches from the nearby woods and deposited them by the fire ring near the side of the lean-to. A few parents had come as well. Two of the fathers and a couple of the kids were already out on the ice, skating around and passing the puck back and forth.

Danny helped gather firewood, and then reluctantly put on his skates. Skating, Danny had concluded, was like a foreign language, something you have to learn early in life for it to feel natural. He stumbled along in little mincing half steps while everybody glided effortlessly around him. Eric tried to give him a few pointers, but it was hopeless. After only a few minutes the arches of his feet started to hurt, and he staggered to the shore to take a break.

Eric came over and sat down beside him. "You could play goalie," he suggested.

"How do I do that?"

"Just try to get in the way of the puck," Eric said. "You don't have to skate much."

"I guess I could try it," Danny said without much enthusiasm.

To his surprise, the game wasn't bad. Danny humiliated himself only a couple of times. Once he tried to pass the puck to a teammate, but instead it dribbled off his stick onto the stick of an opposing player, who immediately poked it past him for a goal. But the other team's goalie wasn't much better, and Danny discovered that he could sometimes prevent a goal by falling down, which came quite naturally to him. Eric scored two goals in the game, and Danny's team won. Afterward there were hot dogs and marshmallows around the fire, and Danny actually felt warm for the first time that weekend, though the temperature just a few feet from the fire was well below freezing.

Danny and Eric walked back toward Eric's house with their skates hanging from hockey sticks over their shoulders. It was four thirty and already dark. But the town was bathed in light. Many of the houses they passed boasted elaborate arrangements of Christmas lights; some had plastic sleighs and reindeer, or scenes of the birth of Jesus. They could see the glow from the lights of the AMIC parking lot, down by the water. And as they turned the corner onto Eric's street, they saw the full Moon, just risen over the harbor, peeking through the bare tree branches.

"Wow," Eric said. "That is one big ol' Moon."

Indeed, it looked as big as it had the night before—bigger, maybe. Danny shivered in the cold, realizing that he had not thought about his father for several hours. He realized it had been a relief not to think about him.

But what was happening out on Harbor Island at this very moment?

"What's the matter?"

Danny became aware that he had stopped walking, and that Eric was looking at him queerly.

He wished he could tell his friend the truth. But he knew he couldn't. It just wasn't something you could tell your friends, that your father was a werewolf—even if it happened to be true.

"Nothing," Danny said. "Do you think the bay's going to freeze over?"

"I've never seen it," Eric said. "It'd be something, though, wouldn't it?"

"Yeah."

"Man, it's cold out here," Eric said after several seconds of silence. He turned toward his house.

"Do you want to come over?" Danny said. "Spend the night at my house?"

"I dunno if my mom'll let me," Eric said. "I'm still in trouble for last week. She'll want to talk to your dad."

"My dad's not home," Danny said.

"What? Where is he?"

"He's, um . . . in New York," Danny said. "He had some kind of meeting, about the screenplay he's working on."

"You mean he's gone for the night?"

"Uh-huh. For a couple of days, actually."

"And he just leaves you guys alone?"

"Sure," Danny said, hoping that he didn't sound too nervous. "Miranda's sixteen, and I'll be fifteen in March. We're too old for baby-sitters."

Eric's face broke out in a grin. "Man, you guys should have a party," he said.

"Yeah." Danny was beginning to regret inviting Eric over. He might show up with a dozen of his friends, trash the house, draw the attention of the cops. He just didn't want to be alone. Why had Miranda abandoned him?

"I gotta go," Eric said. "My mom wants me home before dark. I'll probably catch hell as it is."

"Yeah. I'll see you tomorrow."

Danny went home and turned up the thermostat to seventy-five degrees. His father wasn't there to harp about the oil bill. He heated up the fish sticks and fries and watched the science fiction channel. Every so often he went upstairs to look out at the Moon. The upstairs window was coated with ice crystals. He could hear the weird drumbeats and the sharp, intermittent reports of more ice accumulating on the bay. He thought about calling his mother in

California. But she would hear the worry in his voice and ask him what was wrong, and then he would probably have to tell her. How in the world was he going to be able to sleep?

But he did doze off, on the couch with the TV on. The next thing he knew, he snapped wide awake. Eric was tapping at the window.

"Let me in," his friend called through the glass. He had on a parka with a fur-lined hood pulled around his head so tightly that Danny could barely see his face. Danny got up off the couch and opened the door. A blast of frigid air accompanied Eric through the door.

"What are you doing here?" Danny said. "What time is it, anyway?"

"It's after two," Eric said, pushing back the hood. His cheeks were bright red. "I snuck out. Let's go shoot off some fireworks!"

"Are you crazy? It must be twenty below out there."

Eric pulled off a thick mitten and rubbed his nose. "Yeah, and guess what? The bay's frozen over completely!"

Danny stood there stunned, seconds removed from sleep, unable to immediately comprehend this.

"You can walk on it!" Eric said. "I was just down there myself—I walked all the way around the end of the town docks! It's solid as a rock!"

Understanding finally dawned on Danny. "My God," he exclaimed.

"What?"

But Danny was already past Eric and into his bedroom, opening his closet and the wooden box inside where he kept his fireworks. He gathered the four remaining Power Rockets and scooped up some of the smaller bombs, handing them to Eric, who had followed him into the room and stood behind him. "If these don't scare him off, nothing will," Danny said.

"What?"

"Nothing." Danny pulled on a sweatshirt, and a sweater over that. He stood a moment, then decided to put on a pair of long underwear underneath his jeans. Eric stood at the door of his bedroom, holding fistfuls of fireworks. The furnace hummed madly in the basement.

"Okay, let's go," Danny said. "Oh, wait a minute." He went to the kitchen and grabbed the box of wooden matches from the shelf above the stove. "Okay," he said.

"This is gonna be too cool!" Eric said.

It was unbelievably cold. Danny's nostrils froze instantly. He held the Power Rockets tightly against his chest, zipped inside his parka. The full Moon rode high in the sky, behind the house, obliterating all but the brightest stars. Danny listened for the cracking sound of the ice freezing, and didn't hear it. All was silence.

And then he heard something else. The howl of a wolf.

"Holy shit," Eric said.

Danny stopped. "I forgot something," he said.

"What? You got the matches."

"No, something else," Danny said. "I'll be right back."

"What?" Eric said.

But Danny was already running back toward the house. "Wait for me!" he called over his shoulder. "I'll be right back."

He blew into the house, leaving the door open, not caring about letting the heat out, and went straight to his bedroom, to the chest beside his bed. He opened the top drawer, and there it was—the silver pentagram his father had bought for him in Flagstaff. He wondered where Miranda's was. Was she wearing it? He didn't think so. He thought about going into her room and looking for it, so that he could lend it to Eric for the night, but there wasn't time. His friend was waiting for him outside in the cold.

"Come on," he said to Eric when he rejoined him. They began walking toward town, faster than usual. The pentagram was now around his neck, underneath his layers of clothing.

"Where are we going?" Eric asked.

"AMIC," Danny said. "It's the closest place to the island."

"What? Danny, we can't light these things off down there! They'll catch us for sure!"

"Never mind. Let's just get there." It was almost too cold to talk. Talking wasted precious energy. Danny didn't care if Eric followed him or not. He only knew he had to get there before his father did.

The closest spot on the shore to Harbor Island was the executive parking lot at AMIC. You couldn't drive in there without one of the little plastic cards that opened the gate, but he and Eric were on foot and could simply walk around. The lights were on at the perimeter of the parking lot and at the entrance to the main building, but the place looked deserted in the wee hours of a Sunday morning. They skirted the edge of the parking lot, away from the lights, and lowered themselves over the rocky embankment down to the shore.

Moonlight reflected off a solid sheet of ice between the shore and Harbor Island. And there, far out against the trees of the island, Danny saw something move.

They were far away, but even at that distance he could make out what was happening. The deer skittered out onto the ice, tried to run, lost its footing. The animal in pursuit pounced on it and dragged it down. Sounds seemed magnified in the night. The deer's death screams were faint but clearly audible.

"Holy crap, Danny, that's a wolf!" Eric said, his voice small. "I didn't think there were wolves in Maine."

"Shut up and help me light this thing," Danny said, dropping to one knee and taking a Power Rocket out of his coat. With his mittened hands he scooped out a depression in the pebbly surface of the beach and set the rocket in it. He took off his mitten and fumbled for the matches.

"Are you crazy?" Eric said.

Faint throaty sounds drifted over the ice from the kill, and Danny looked out. The wolf-creature raised its head and bayed at the Moon. Danny felt the hair on the back of his neck prickle despite the cold. And then the beast stood up on its hind legs and moved out onto the ice, toward the mainland.

"Oh, no!" Danny breathed into the frigid air.

"What *is* that thing?" Eric squeaked.

"Quick!" Danny said. "Stand back." He lit the fuse on the Power Rocket.

It soared into the air, did a loop, and exploded, raining sparkling balls of gunpowder down onto the ice. The beast stopped, growled, looked right at them. It stood there, silhouetted in the moonlight. And then it dropped to all fours and walked, as though stalking its next victim, toward the shore and the bright lights of the AMIC credit card company. Toward the very spot where they were standing.

"I can't believe this," Eric breathed.

Danny pulled out another rocket and began preparing another divot to launch it from.

"Danny, let's get out of here," Eric said.

"We've got to scare him off," Danny said between clenched teeth. "Here." He handed Eric the Power Rocket, went for the matches.

"Danny, someone's gonna see us!"

"Someone's gonna *die* if we let that thing get to town," Danny said. "Aim it low. Aim it right at him."

"Danny—"

"Never mind! Here." Danny grabbed the Power Rocket, set it at a low angle, lit a match. Touched the match to the fuse. The rocket took off, looped once, then crashed into the ice less than twenty feet from the creature, where it lay sizzling. The animal kept coming toward them. A moment later the rocket exploded. The wolf jumped to one side, but it did not stop, or increase its loping pace. It just kept coming.

"Shit!" Danny spat. He looked around frantically. His eyes seized on some dried brush and driftwood by the base of the bank. "We've got to light a fire," he said.

"Are you nuts?" Eric cried. "Somebody's probably already seen the fireworks. The cops are gonna be here any minute!"

Danny pulled out the last two Power Rockets. He handed one to Eric. "Light this off," he said. "And here." He reached into his pockets and handed his friend several small bombs the size of caramels. "These make a lot of noise," he said. "Light them off too." He knelt to prepare his last rocket.

Eric just stood there.

"Well, come on!"

Eric didn't move. Danny touched the match to the end of the fuse.

"Danny, I think we should get out of here." But Eric wasn't looking at him when he said this. He was looking out onto the ice at the wolf, which had stopped about a hundred yards away and was now looking back at them. It had seen them for sure.

"Goddamn it, give me those!"

Danny tried to grab the small bombs from his friend, but Eric pushed him away. "Keep your hands off me!" Eric cried.

Danny staggered backward, losing his footing. The Power Rocket ignited just as he stumbled into it. The rocket flew upward, away from the shore, did a nifty loop-de-loop, and crashed through a window of AMIC's main building.

The shattering of glass stunned the two boys and the wolf. All three looked at one another. An alarm went off, louder than the fireworks. Then there was an explosion from somewhere inside the building.

"That's it," Eric said. "I'm out of here."

But the animal on the ice had not moved. Danny took two steps toward it.

"Christ's sake, Danny, come on!"

"He won't hurt me," Danny said.

"It's a wolf, man!"

"He won't hurt me," Danny repeated. "He's my father." He took two more steps out onto the ice.

"Man, you are *disturbed,* you know that? Screw this, I'm out of here!" And without waiting for a reply from Danny, Eric scrambled up the bank and took off running down the street.

Smoke poured from the broken window in AMIC's main building, and then suddenly there were flames. Danny guessed that the fiery balls that Power Rockets shot off, which looked so pretty high above the ground, must have scattered all around inside the office, setting stuff on fire. The alarm wailed. Out on the ice the werewolf stood its ground as Danny walked toward it. Closer—now Danny could see the flames reflected in its eyes. He looked quickly back over his shoulder. Flames filled the windows. In a moment the whole building would be engulfed. Cops and firefighters would be all over the place. He hoped Eric would have time to get away.

The werewolf crouched low as he approached. Then it stood up on its hind legs. It was easily as tall as a man, easily as tall as his father. It *was* his father, Danny reminded himself, and he prayed that something of his father's essential being remained in the beast's consciousness.

Danny searched the canine face for some hint of humanity. There was blood on the elongated snout from the killing of the deer. The beast bared its teeth at him. Danny stopped. "Dad," he said, "you have to get out of here. They'll kill you if they see you."

The werewolf crouched, and in that moment Danny anticipated his own death, for he was certain the creature was about to spring on him and tear him to pieces. He was not afraid. It had to end, sometime, somehow. He felt the heat of the flames behind him.

Slowly Danny reached inside his sweater, inside the layers of shirts and sweatshirt, and removed the pentagram from around his neck. He dangled it in front of the beast. The silver star inside the silver circle caught the moonlight, caught the reflection from the flames. The werewolf dropped to all fours and backed slowly away.

"Go," Danny said. "Go, before they find you."

The beast emitted a low, gutteral howl that came out more of a whine. It backed slowly away from Danny, then turned and bounded across the ice toward the sleeping center of town, toward the silent theater and the silvery hulk of the fish-packing factory.

The fire had melted away a swath of ice next to the shore. Danny could not get back the way he had come. He was still standing out on the ice in the middle of the harbor when he heard the sirens approaching.

TWELVE

Later Danny remembered his arrest like a blur. But the fire! He did not know what AMIC's main building was made of—compressed credit card bills, maybe—but it went up like a barbecue grill when someone's dumped too much lighter fluid on it. The flames lit up the whole sky and the black smoke blotted out the Moon. By daybreak nothing was left of the building but the charred hulks of computers and chairs and desks and paper shredders and a pile of smoldering black rubble.

The cop who arrested him kept asking him where his parents were. Danny told him he didn't know. What was he supposed to say? "My mother's in California and my father's a werewolf." The cop was pissed off enough already.

"How old are you, son?" he growled.

"Fourteen," Danny mumbled.

"And you don't know where your parents are? They don't know where you are?"

Danny shook his head, and the cop shook his.

He was taken to a holding cell at the county jail. They took his fingerprints and his picture, one facing the camera and one in profile, just like on TV. They took the stuff in his pockets, as well as the pentagram. One cop turned it over and over in his fat, clumsy fingers, frowning, but nobody said anything about it. They interrogated him for something like three hours, in a room with a large metal table and not much else. Three cops alternately acted like his friend and threatened him with adult prison. They had already told him he had the right to remain silent, and that's mostly what he did, no matter how much they yelled at him. They tried to frighten him, and they did, a little, but they didn't know how scared Danny had been out on the ice, facing down the beast that was his father. He did not tell them anything, and there was nothing they could do to make him tell them.

The holding cell had only a hard bunk in it, with no sheets. There was a grate in one corner for him to piss in. Danny asked if he could have something to read and they just laughed. Finally he started singing "A Hundred Bottles of Beer on the Wall" to himself, as slowly and melodically as he could, and when he was finished, he wished he'd started at two hundred. He tried to think of all the countries in the world that started with the letter *A*—Albania, Algeria, Argentina, and so on. He went all the way through the alphabet, to Zaire and Zambia and Zimbabwe. After what seemed like three days but was probably no more than three hours, his father and sister showed up. The guards made Miranda wait in the hall, but they let Ken into the cell and left them alone.

Danny's father looked okay. He'd had a chance to clean up, and the only signs of fatigue were the purplish bags beneath both eyes. They sat on the bed and talked in low voices. Danny wondered if their conversation was being monitored.

"It's gone," Danny's father said. "The whole building—burnt right to the ground. You do that?"

"I guess so," Danny said. "I didn't mean to."

"We'll get you out of here," his father said.

"Dad, what about you?" Danny said.

"What do you mean?"

"Do you remember anything? Out on the ice? Me?"

Danny's father shook his head. "I woke up behind the cannery. There wasn't anybody around. All the action was down by the fire." He stopped and looked at Danny. "You saw me, huh?"

Danny nodded, looking at the floor.

"And you tried to scare me off?"

Danny nodded again.

"Did anybody else see me?"

Danny shook his head. "No," he murmured.

"Good," his father said.

Silence fell between them. Danny thought of Eric, and wondered what, if anything, he would say to his friends at school, his parents. Maybe nothing. He hoped nothing. Maine kids seemed to have a sense of when to keep their mouths shut. If Eric didn't incriminate himself, no one would ever need to know that he had been there. But he had seen the werewolf.

And Danny thought he remembered saying, "It's my father." Or was he only imagining that, as he reconstructed the scene in his mind? He knew one thing for sure. He had looked his father in the eye, out there on the ice, and his father had recognized him.

"I had to get home," Ken said finally. "I didn't have a coat or anything. And I didn't want to be seen. I thought it was strange you guys weren't home, but I didn't know you had anything to do with the fire until I got out of the shower and the cops called."

"Dad, what about tonight?" Danny asked. "Isn't there another night of full moon?"

"Yeah. But it's clouding up. It's already a lot warmer. They said on the radio there's some weather moving in from the south. Might snow, even."

"Lucky," Danny said.

"Yeah," his father agreed.

"Especially since I can't take you to the island."

Another moment of awkward silence passed.

Then Ken said, "Danny, I'll do whatever it takes to get you out of here. I'll tell them what I am, if that's what I have to do. Only . . ."

"Only what, Dad?"

"I'm more help to you on the outside. If I tell them that I'm a werewolf, and that you burned down AMIC by accident trying to protect me, they're liable to throw me in a nuthouse and you in adult prison."

Danny started to say something, but his father held up his hand. "I know you're only fourteen," he said. "But they can charge you as an adult if they want. If that security guard hadn't made it out of the building, they probably would. They might anyway. That's why we've got to get you a good lawyer. I can do that, on the outside. I can't do it from the booby hatch."

Danny nodded. He understood. And that's when he made up his mind that no lawyer was going to hear a word from him about werewolves.

"Your sister wants to say hello." Danny's father stood up and went to the door of the cell. A uniformed officer appeared and let him out. A moment later Miranda materialized on the other side of the bars. She managed a thin, sympathetic smile. Danny reached a hand through and their fingers touched.

"I leave you alone for one night, and you burn down the AMIC corporation," she said.

"It was an accident," Danny told her. "Besides, I'm sure they've got the best insurance money can buy."

"It was an ugly building anyway," Miranda said. "Looked out of place on the harbor. I hope you remembered to bring marshmallows."

Danny laughed. It felt good to laugh.

"Remember when you told Dad you wanted to be a lawyer?" he asked his sister. "Do you remember what he said?"

Miranda nodded and smiled without effort. "He said I had the right name for it. Because Miranda is what they call it when—"

"I got it," Danny said. "I got the Miranda speech. 'You have the right to remain silent' and all that. Just like on TV."

"I wouldn't go bragging about it," his sister said. But she squeezed his hand before she left and told him to hang in there.

They transferred him to the Eastern Maine Juvenile Detention Center the following day, the day before Christmas, the day he was supposed to have picked his father up on Harbor Island after the full moon had safely passed. They served turkey and stuffing and cranberry sauce in the cafeteria, and his father and sister came to visit. They reported that the temperature had risen to forty degrees and it was raining. The ice in the harbor was breaking up and drifting out to sea. They brought presents: a radio and CD player with headphones, a few of his favorite CDs, and about ten books. "You can open your other presents when you get out," Ken said. "And you *will* get out."

Danny went into court two days after Christmas. He was represented by a portly, silver-haired attorney named Sam Mitchell, whom his father had hired because Danny knew the lawyer's son at school. Mitchell made it clear from the outset that he did not approve of either Danny's affection for fireworks or his father's hands-off style of supervision. "It's lucky for you nobody died," he huffed at their first meeting around a metal table in a tiny little room at the

211

courthouse. "If anyone had been trapped in there, you'd be looking at years, even at your age." Danny didn't think the lawyer liked him much. Fat, wealthy lawyers had little use for teenage hoodlums.

On Mitchell's advice, Danny said just two words: "Not guilty." Bail was set at fifty thousand dollars, which some AMIC customers, his father said, could charge off on their credit cards without a second thought. It was hopelessly out of his father's reach, however, and so Danny sat in jail. He read, he listened to music, and he talked to the other prisoners as little as possible. His father and sister came to visit almost every day.

Danny's case made the front page of both local papers and the *Bangor Daily News*. The fire had been visible for a hundred miles, the newspapers said. A security guard had been taken to the hospital for smoke inhalation, and a bunch of people had lost their jobs, at least temporarily, but the company had already begun cleaning up the mess along the shorefront and was planning to rebuild. Meanwhile Danny sat in jail.

He saw the glow from the New Year's fireworks through the tiny window, high up the wall in his concrete cell. Faintly, in the distance, he heard their crackling and booming reports. *There it is,* he thought. *Midnight. The year 2000.* He had never in his wildest dreams imagined that when the world's odometer turned, he would be in jail.

His sister and his father were probably watching from their living room. Maybe they had braved the cold and joined the crowd downtown. Danny couldn't imagine why the people of Liverpool would want to watch fireworks after the show he had given them.

I did that, Danny thought. *I burned down Assholes of Maine in Cubicles. What a mess I'm in.*

Already someone had written a letter to one of the newspapers comparing him to the kids who shot up schools and the guy who blew up the building in Oklahoma City. Which Danny knew was preposterous. He had never even held a gun in his hand. His father had never allowed one in the house. Sam Mitchell was trying to get the charge knocked back from arson to malicious mischief, plus possession of illegal fireworks. He wanted to play up the accident angle, but Danny could tell that he didn't entirely believe his story. "You've got to level with me, son," he said. "If I'm going to be able to help you, you need to tell me everything."

Right, Danny thought. *If he only knew.*

But Danny knew that burning AMIC down had not stopped the lunar cycle, and sooner or later, before the third week of January, his father and Miranda would have to come up with a plan to avoid a murderous rampage through the streets of Liverpool. He knew he couldn't help from jail, but that didn't stop him from brooding about it as he lay on his hard bunk through the long winter nights. His father should be the one locked up, he thought bitterly. It was hard not to resent him in those long, dark hours. In his conscious mind Danny knew that it wasn't his father's fault, that he hadn't asked for any of this. One night it occurred to him that if Dad got on a plane and kept flying west, around the world for three days, he could avoid the full moon entirely. Sure, if he had money and could charter a plane, he could conceivably do that. But Danny realized that while he was the one in jail, his father lived in a prison of sorts too.

THIRTEEN

"'The corporate world must be brought to its knees and smashed.'"

"Huh?"

"That's my dad talking," Danny said.

Paul leaned on the handle of his floor mop and nodded—not, Danny thought, because he understood, but just to be friendly. It had snowed the previous night—the first snow of the winter though it was already January—and wet, muddy boot prints covered the white linoleum hall between the cells. Danny wished he could go out and play in it. Snow was novel to him—in California he had seen it in the mountains, where it attracted carloads of people from the city and melted within a few days. To Paul it was just another mess to clean up.

Two guards came through the corridor, in winter coats and big boots, tracking slush all over the part of the floor that Paul had just mopped. "Lotta snow out there, Paulie," one of them said, clapping him on the shoulder as they passed. They continued down the corridor, ignoring Danny and the kids in the other cells. Near the far door one of them said something to the other and they both laughed. When they were gone, Paul began cleaning up their trail.

"Assholes," Danny said.

Paul said nothing.

Danny liked talking to Paul, because Paul was the only person who talked to Danny about anything other than his crime and what kind of punishment he would possibly get. He mopped the floors and brought lunch and did other menial chores around the place. Paul wasn't a guard, because he didn't wear a uniform and order the prisoners around like the other guards did. Some of the kids made fun of him. He was tall and slow moving and he had dark, bristly hair that stood straight up off his head in about three places. He was a young guy, about twenty-five, and he wasn't the sharpest tool in the shed, as Danny's grandfather used to say. He was slow to understand things, and he didn't seem to know when the guards were teasing him. Like they would ask him about his wife and kids, and he didn't have a wife and kids. Danny had heard that he was related to the warden somehow, and that was how he got his job. Some of the kids did things like pissing on the floor so he'd have to clean it up. Or they'd say, "I ordered ham and cheese on rye," when he brought them the usual lunch of bologna on white bread with an orange and sometimes a chocolate chip cookie. "You forgot the fruit salad, Paul," they'd yell at him. "Where the hell's my fruit salad?" Danny knew it was all harmless bullshit because jail was so boring, but it struck him as kind of mean, and he tried to be nice to Paul whenever he could.

Paul never once asked him what he was in for. Danny was grateful for that, because everyone else seemed to want information from him. He had been interrogated by cops, psychiatrists, even other juvenile delinquents. At first they'd put him in a cell with a kid who claimed to have stolen several cars. The guy wouldn't shut up. He kept after Danny about how he'd managed to burn down a whole credit card company, and Danny had finally punched him. That had landed him in the shrink's office and finally in a cell by himself. The psychiatrist had told Danny he was being uncooperative, and Danny had just shrugged. What was he going to do, tell him the truth?

Danny preferred a single cell anyway. His father had brought him some more books and his Game Boy, and he spent most of his time lying on his bunk either reading or playing. Most of the kids in jail were real losers, kids he wouldn't have hung out with on the outside, and most of them were in for really stupid stuff, like breaking into stores or selling drugs at school. One kid threw a rock through the windshield of a cop car. How stupid was that? Even in jail, where you didn't have any choice, a lot of them were still too thick to shut up and do what they were told.

But Danny had also discovered that some of the guards treated him with something that almost amounted to respect, and he had an idea it had something to do with the crime of which he was accused. He knew a lot of people in Liverpool didn't like AMIC.

There were fights sometimes, but Danny stayed out of them. After he had punched that one kid, the others knew he would stick up for himself, and they left him alone. Most of the fights were about dumb things anyway, like what TV show to watch in the lounge or the rules of a card game. And there was no faster way to get in trouble with the guards than to start a fight. Guards weren't like teachers. They didn't put up with much.

"How much snow is out there now?" Danny asked.

"Must be more'n a foot," Paul said. "She was still coming down hard when I come in."

"Man. That's a lot of snow."

"This ain't nothin'," Paul said. "This is just normal stuff. You should've been here a couple a years ago, when we had that ice storm. Now *that* was bad."

"I've heard about it," Danny said. "All those bent-over trees—that's what did it, right?"

"Yup. Two years, and you can still see the damage it did."

Danny had, in fact, heard about that ice storm while still in California. It had made national news, and every time Maine had been mentioned in the newspaper in San Diego, his father had pointed it out. He had quickly forgotten about it. But in Maine, two years after the fact, the storm still had the status of legend.

"Whole state lost power," Paul said. "Some people went without electricity for two weeks. We had to use the emergency generators. Man, that was some storm." He shook his head, remembering. "Yuh could hear trees crashing all over the place, big branches snapping right off. Every so often yuh'd see sparks in the distance, and yuh knew another transformer had blown out somewhere. It was somethin' else."

"So I heard," Danny said.

"What happened is it rained, and then when the temperature dropped it turned to sleet and then froze," Paul said. "So everything got coated in ice, like an inch thick. And that much ice, it's wicked heavy. Dragged down power lines, snapped poles right in half. Took a long time to clean it up. People couldn't live in their homes, 'cause there weren't no power."

"But AMIC came to the rescue, right?"

Paul nodded as he ran the mop over the linoleum. "They got generators too."

"I know," Danny said. "My dad says they brag about it."

"I tell yuh, they helped out a lot of folks. Everyone else was out of power, but they was all warm and lit up. They opened up half of that big building as an emergency shelter."

"Probably the only time anyone was allowed in there without a drug test and a badge," Danny said.

"They been good for this town," Paul said.

"Yeah," Danny agreed. "Just not for me and my family. I wish we'd stayed in California."

Paul kept on mopping the floor and didn't say anything else. Pretty soon he was out of easy conversation range down the hall, and Danny settled back on his bunk. He wondered if his father and sister would make it in through the snow to visit him. Nobody else had any visitors.

Danny picked up the book he was reading, a science fiction novel by Arthur C. Clarke, and tried to get involved in the story. But all he could think of was that the first full moon of 2000 was less than three weeks away, and there was nothing he could do about it.

He hadn't even gotten through a chapter when Paul came back and tapped on the bars. "Someone's here to see you," he said.

"Really?" Danny sat up. "I thought you said there was a blizzard outside."

But there they were—both father and lawyer. They jumped to their feet when Paul and the guard led him into the visitors' room. His father gave him a hug. Sam Mitchell stood there, lightly drumming his fingers on the tabletop next to his opened briefcase. He was smiling.

"I think we might have some good news," the lawyer said.

Danny looked back and forth between the two men. "Yeah?" he said. "Let's hear it."

Mitchell extended his arm toward a chair at the end of the table, indicating that Danny should sit. He did. His father and his lawyer took chairs on opposite sides.

"I've been in touch with AMIC's lawyers,"

Mitchell said. "They're a tough bunch, but they have indicated a willingness to be reasonable." He drummed his fingers again.

"What's that mean?" Danny asked.

"It means AMIC's corporate lawyers in Delaware have considered the potential adverse effect on the company's public image of throwing the book at a fourteen-year-old kid who might have burned down their building by accident."

"*Might* have? It *was* an accident!"

"Well, that's your story, and I respect you for sticking to it," the lawyer said. His smile did not change. "You can understand, I think, why the heads of AMIC's Liverpool division might feel differently."

Danny looked at his father, who looked at his hands. "They think I did it on *purpose?*" he said.

Mitchell and his father exchanged glances. "Something of that nature did come up in my discussion with AMIC's lawyers," Sam Mitchell said.

Danny shook his head and smiled for the first time. A simple yes would have conveyed the same message. He loved the way lawyers used words as insulation, padding their sentences with extra syllables so that the essence of what they meant, while still there, didn't poke anybody with its sharp edges.

"They're willing to consider a plea bargain," the lawyer said. "They're willing to drop the arson and let you plead down to the fireworks charge, plus criminal tresspass, provided you agree to certain conditions of probation."

Danny looked at his father, who suddenly discovered something fascinating on the ceiling. What was going on here?

"If you agree to what they're asking," Sam Mitchell continued, "it means we can probably get you out of here early next week."

"What do they want?" Danny asked.

"Six hundred hours of community service. Spent under the supervision of the AMIC corporation, at their new office complex up on Route One in Liverpool."

Danny sat silently for several seconds. "You mean, they want me to *work* for them?" he asked when no one spoke.

The lawyer bit his lower lip and nodded. "At

the completion of which," he said, "all charges will be dismissed. You'll be on probation until you're eighteen. And you won't be paid, of course."

Danny didn't know what to say. So this was their plan to get him out of jail. No wonder his father wouldn't look at him.

"Six hundred hours," he said. "That'll take me—"

"At ten hours a week, plus school vacations, a little over a year."

Danny turned to his father. "So you sold me to AMIC, huh?"

"Danny, please . . ."

"And I get to work alongside you, right?"

His father looked away. Sam Mitchell's fingers drummed the table again.

"Danny, they fired me," his father said. "Remember, I wasn't supposed to miss any more days? Most people in the building you burned will get their jobs back in a couple of months. Not me."

Danny looked at his hands, and then up at Sam Mitchell. "I'd like to talk it over with my dad alone," he said.

"By all means."

Mitchell snapped his briefcase shut and stood up. "I'll be right outside," he said, and left the room.

"I'm sorry you got fired," Danny said.

"I'm not," his father replied. "I hated that job. And I hated the hours. Not good hours for a werewolf."

"Was this your idea?" Danny asked his father.

Ken looked at him at last. "Are you kidding?" he said. "No, it wasn't my idea, or Sam's. It's something AMIC came up with."

"Generous of them," Danny said.

"Yeah. Of course they're only doing it to make themselves look good."

"I'm going to do it," Danny said.

"I don't see that you have much choice," his father said. "It may be slavery, but it beats the hell out of jail."

"You can't fight the corporate world, Dad."

"No, I guess not," he said. He looked at his hands. Danny saw that the fingernail on his right index finger was turning black. The sign of the wolf.

"Tell Mr. Mitchell to accept their offer," Danny said.

His father nodded. "It'll be good to get you out of here," he said.

"You're telling me! You don't have to eat the slop they serve here."

His father laughed, and Danny laughed with him.

"So what are you going to do now?" Danny asked his father.

Ken looked at him and raised an eyebrow. "That's the other piece of good news," he said. "I got a call from Dale, my agent, last night. He's got a producer in L.A. who wants to option my screenplay."

"Which one?"

"*Riders of the Purple Dawn*. And the guy wants to see the new one as soon as it's done. He's cutting a check for five thousand dollars. So screw AMIC and their corporate bullshit. I'm just sorry they've got you in their clutches now."

"That's great, Dad," Danny said. "It really is. But what about the other thing?"

"What about it?"

"Full moon's in what? Another eleven days?"

227

"I've been talking to Sid in Pismo Beach," his father said. "He seems to think we might be able to construct a cage in our basement strong enough to hold me, for when we can't use the island. You guys could go visit your grandparents, or friends, just to be safe."

"It sounds risky, Dad. What if someone hears you, and calls the cops?"

"Well, Sid's also been experimenting with some herbal sedatives, which he thinks may counteract the effect, or at least render me harmless while I'm in the werewolf state. He said he put some stuff in the mail for me, some dried herbs and recipes. But he advised me to continue using the island whenever I can. Just to be safe."

Danny started to protest, but his father cut him off. "All the stuff's still out there, in the cave," he said. "And as you can see, I didn't freeze to death. I'll be all right."

"But what if the bay freezes over again?"

Danny's father smiled thinly. "That's a chance we'll have to take," he said. "Besides, it probably won't happen again for another fifty years."